NO ONE YOU KNOW

**STRANGERS AND
THE STORIES WE TELL**

JASON SCHWARTZMAN

Outpost19 | San Francisco
outpost19.com

Schwartzman, Jason
No One You Know/ Jason Schwartzman

ISBN 9781944853761 (pbk)
ISBN 9781944853808 (ebk)

Library of Congress Control Number: 2020950887

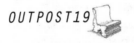

OUTPOST19

ORIGINAL PROVOCATIVE READING
SAN FRANCISCO | @OUTPOST19

THE STORIES IN
NO ONE YOU KNOW
ARE ALL TRUE

SOME NAMES
HAVE BEEN CHANGED
TO PROTECT
INDIVIDUALS' PRIVACY

To Michelle, Paul, and Evan

JASON SCHWARTZMAN

"What you don't know about me
is still my life."

– Aleksandar Hemon
The Lazarus Project

TABLE OF CONTENTS

I

I

THE SHAPE OF A STORY

"Bit 'im in the jugular," the truck driver tells me about the bear ten feet away, describing the day the bear went crazy. I'm working on the set of a low-budget boxing film on the city's industrial edge. Today they're filming a dream sequence, and it's cold and rainy. I can't see the bear, but his padlocked trailer is shaking right in front of us.

The shoot is almost done; there is just this bear between us and completion. A 300-pound bear that once attacked his own trainer for no discernible reason. His "best friend," according to the truck driver. Do bears need reasons? I am standing on the elevated step outside the truck door so I can get one step farther away from the bear. Through a square porthole I can actually see the bars of his steel cage. The driver is cueing up the attack video on YouTube. It is very early in the morning, but he is smoking a celebratory cigar for an obscure personal victory. Or maybe this is just how he begins his day.

At first, the bear and his trainer are playing. It seems light and friendly, but soon enough the one-inch bear on the iPhone goes berserk and lunges at the trainer's throat; I have to look away. Even though the truck driver told me what was coming, I can't quite believe it. There is no cue, no transition – it is clearly not a movie scene. What was half a joke hardens into something more real, the man stumbling off screen clutching his bloody neck.

The trailer shakes again.

"I don't understand why they don't put a bear

down. They'll put a dog down," the truck driver says, agreeing with me that it's upsetting and strange this same bear will appear on the set – that he is still eligible for a scene-stealing cameo.

·

I have never seen the set itself. I'm a hired hand assisting craft services on days when there are more extras than usual. I am possibly the lowest person on the tall totem pole of the film – a temp's temp. It started off as a not-so-bad way to make a little extra cash, but at some point I have to admit that these little side jobs are consuming more and more of my life. It's hard to remember the stuff you thought you were good at when you're on your knees in the back of a van buried in sacks of Sweet'N Low and wrapped in an enormous fur coat someone lent you because you underdressed. Your grip loosens on the story you used to tell yourself.

Maybe it is also the fact that there are people pretending, that everyone is an actor, or the fact that the crew members are constantly saying Real Barbara and Real Bob, like we all have two selves.

The boxing film is "based" on a true story, turns out.

·

We are instructed not to bring honey today. Usually we set up right outside the restaurant's entrance, but today we are banished all the way around a corner. Outside is *away* from the cameras. Outside is jokes, breaks, cigarettes. We brew the coffee, pour out the candy, slice the bread – we are the ones who sate the overworked and the stressed.

"Any bennies in there?" someone asks me about the M&Ms.

With the staff's hunger comes news of the bear – he is already inside. Apparently this is the bear's second entrance, since he had to be led in before anyone arrived. A dress rehearsal so he could get used to the environment, so the pathway would seem familiar before all the humans came with their cameras and lights and voices. Apparently the murderer of his best friend likes marshmallows. Fruit loops too.

"Did you see it?" everyone asks me, meaning the bear, not the video.

Word is that the bear is very sweet; his interests include walking in circles, having his neck scratched. He travels with a companion female bear, who soothes him. I ask a Serbian woman I sometimes chat with to describe the bear to me, to those of us outside who do not merit the privilege of seeing the bear firsthand.

"Why would I do that when I can just show you the picture?"

The picture just looks like a bear. It's static, so I learn nothing about this particular bear who is supposed to brawl with the boxer. Unable to see the real thing, I at least want the story. I always thought a pleasure of stories was to feel close to something that's actually far away, an illusion of proximity.

Due to my penchant for thinking about these kinds of things, someone calls me The Philosopher. I embrace this new identity. I dress myself up in it.

"They call me The Philosopher around here," I tell everyone.

Someone mentions a lousy bear he once worked with that was supposed to be scary but kept getting scared. We are vanned to a church basement for lunch and a girl with a septum piercing shows me a video of the bear on set. He seems surprisingly playful and cute, but I feel compelled to tell her about the bear's history. About the jugular.

"Don't you know?" I ask.

•

These frequent but marginal exchanges begin to feel like stray thoughts moving through a consciousness. One crew member has been obsessing about zombies all day. He asks aloud what zombies are a metaphor for. What do they mean?

I mention some theories: mindless consumerism, immigration, etc. Later he walks through again, his zombie questions veering into thoughts about himself, and what he thinks the zombie movies are about: being you but not you.

"Don't you ever say something or do something and wonder: 'Why'd I do that?'" he asks forlornly.

It sounds like maybe he heard the rumor of the murderous bear too, and it conjured a dark memory. An ill-conceived affair. A mean-spirited message he sent.

I try to toss in my two cents and set his mind at ease. "Of course!" That's something that is actually very human, I say. Not being consistent. Not always knowing. But he isn't really listening to me. He looks expectantly at a higher-ranking crew member.

"Uhhh, no," the guy answers emphatically.

•

The Serbian woman tells me that she grew up with bears, owing to an eccentric father who reminds me of a John Irving protagonist. She's on her break, one cigarette after another, and she shows me the pictures to prove it.

They named the bears Meda and Medita. Boy and girl in Serbian. She also says she's from Iowa — it seems unexpected but possible, the old waves of European immigration to the Midwest. I mention one of my Iowa bits, that, like some of the Midwest, you can recognize it by the perfect gridded regularity of the region when seen from above, sized for crops. She gets confused and the jig is up. Then a confession: she has never had any bears.

Is that what happens on a set? The proximity to a larger fiction inspiring smaller ones? Everyone fancying herself a storyteller? Or is it just what happens anywhere, inventing yourself over and over again?

At first I like the anonymity of the job, but over the course of the day, I crave shreds of recognition. That I am not just this. That there is more to me than subpar kiwi slicing.

"I'm an editor," I tell someone when they ask. "A writer."

Sure I am, but I am this other thing, too.

She calls me a "double agent."

It hits the spot.

Calling everything "material" as a way to comfort yourself.

•

Instead of complaining about the weather, conversations about *Grizzly Man* are substitute pleasantries. Werner Herzog tried to make it seem like a mystery, but really it was simple, some guy says. Dude showed up at the wrong time of year, when there were no more salmon. If the bears have their salmon, he said, you can walk right up to them.

"He didn't have food so he became food. They're not stupid – they remember."

Bits of the YouTube video nag me all day, seemingly preloaded for my spare minutes. I never get to see the bear with my own eyes though – I don't even know he's gone until someone tells me.

During the long stretches of downtime, I am still talking about the bear, wondering about it, and someone tells me the truck driver is a liar, is just pulling my leg.

"I saw a man die," I tell him, awkwardly attached to the idea.

Somehow it feels like something is being taken away. With all this downtime to think, I wonder if I latched onto the legend as a kind of narrative ticket, an outsider's way of sneaking inside the set I was never allowed to visit. Tired of being on the periphery of things. Of moving to a new borough and knowing no one. Of always missing the heart of the matter.

What a magical thing: a bear in New York City. The skyscrapers his forest. The fur and the steel. A wonder.

•

We have second meal and I am chatting with the PAs. There is not much left for us to do. It is sinking in that I was likely duped by the mischievous truck driver, that the video bear was another bear queued up from a basic YouTube search.

As I think more about it, I realize that maybe the man in the video didn't even die. I feel relieved. The narrative possibilities are spinning, spinning, spinning.

Another PA sits down and we talk about the rumor of the bear. About how I believed the story.

"It's probably true," this second PA says, to my surprise.

Someone sitting nearby wonders aloud why the bear isn't in jail for what he did.

"He already is," the first PA says.

•

"That's the *real* boxer," people whisper when the man on whom the movie is based shows up.

Everyone wants a picture with him, an anecdote, a shred of this man they can peel off and slap somewhere on the virtual walls of their life. I am no different. It feels like a personal messiah has arrived. I endure the special pleasure of having my hand crushed by his.

"What's the secret of boxing?" I ask him, sliding back into reporter mode.

"Training. Conditioning," he says, "but it doesn't hurt to have a 20-inch neck."

He is Chuck Wepner, a famous bruising long shot, one of only four people who actually knocked down Muhammad Ali. So tough they called him the Bayonne Bleeder. The guy could bleed out a million quarts and still stand. No one was able to knock him out, not once.

"Never been stopped yet," he told me, now an older man.

As it happened, a then-obscure actor named Sylvester Stallone watched his 1975 title bout against Ali from across the country in LA. He wrote a screenplay based on Wepner's life which became *Rocky,* one of the most successful movie franchises of all time. Wepner never saw a cent, though.

Later I read in an interview that he used to falsely claim he got paid $70,000 because he was embarrassed. It was *his life* and he got nothing?

It doesn't seem to bother him anymore. Maybe because he's finally getting his own movie, or maybe he just got over it. Still, I can't help but notice he keeps a thick wad of photographs inside his jacket pocket, secured with a rubber band. He's a sweet man. All he wants to do is show everyone his pictures. Here he is with Celebrity A, with Politician B.

Here he is with a bear. They actually fought, once upon a time.

Wepner gives me his card, which lists various achievements and the phone number for the liquor store he owns. I look it over, feeling like some kind of kin. All of us clutching our own myths. Some true, some less true, all ours in the end.

"Inspiration for Rocky Movies," his card says.

II

WHAT IS YOUR NAME, BY THE WAY?

"How much those chicken fingers cost?"

"Four dollars, I think. Good deal. You been to Derby Day before?"

"If I'm livin' I come. Same spot every time. Vets like gambling since it's not so different. All the excitement, then it's slow. Hard to readjust to society. I got some help, now I'm sane."

"Where did you serve?"

"Vietnam. Every five years I get something in the mail about a reunion, but everyone's dead. I went with young boys who knew about killin' but never done it. When you kill someone, there's that second before you shoot 'em. You're frozen. Couldn't sleep for days. Sergeant tells you if you don't kill him he'll kill you, then one day you're the sergeant, and you tell people that."

DISTANCE

From far off, I see a solitary figure coming toward me — the distance gives us time to contemplate each other. It is the Detroitness too, this feeling that there are not many other people around. The tall beige buildings have shed their glass, the windows just rectangles of black. I am trying to return to the hostel, my camera around my neck, my laptop in my backpack containing every-thing I've ever written. On a red brick wall nearby there are two black arrows pointing in different directions. One arrow is captioned: "This Way To Lose." The other arrow says: "This Way To Die." I am constantly compar-ing this city to St. Louis, giving it the short end of the stick. But it isn't quite fair: I spent so much time there and am just a visitor here — a tourist with one quick view. The guy comes into focus and I can tell he is homeless or very poor by the dirt streaks on his clothes. As he drifts closer, I can see him eyeing my camera.

He gestures rapidly with frenetic hand motions while my heart thumps. He is going to rob me and there's nothing I can do. There is no one even within earshot — it has been minutes and avenues since I saw another human being. And then I understand. He's deaf and he's signing, asking me to take his picture. He sees I'm not from here, that I'm trying to photograph Detroit. When I think of Detroit, I think of weedy lawns and the rubble within the Packard Plant. I think of the spectral train sta-tion.

Maybe he's thinking, "Hey — I'm Detroit, too."

The man gives me his biggest smile and I take his picture. He starts signing again: "I'm hungry," I think he's saying, but it's hard to know. Maybe he hopes I can help him get something to eat. I angle myself away, I think I have some singles, but "Fuck it," I think, "I'll just give him a 20." The Detroitness. If the circumstances were slightly different, it could easily be my own ransom note, but I hand the money over without a word. He takes it, sees it — he is so surprised he cries out.

His hands are moving faster now, complicated patterns in the space between us. I can't understand any nuance beyond the obvious joy; the only word I know in sign language is the gesture for divorce, two fingers together and parallel, and then moving apart, slowly, until the speaker's arms have reached their limits, the two people already transported to opposite ends of the earth.

He can't stop smiling.

We fist bump and I walk away, but after a few steps I look over my shoulder — I can feel the suspicion still in me like a toxin. I want to make sure he isn't following me, that he hasn't decided he wants more where the money came from. I am naturally a little guarded, but I wonder if the suspicion is me or if it is me in this city.

I look back and he's in the same spot — he hasn't moved an inch. He's still smiling, signing, saying something I wish I could hear.

THE PLACE WHERE
SHE CAN BE HERSELF

"Is this day over yet?" the customer asks.

It is 1:30 p.m.

No one knows what to say. Not the owner. Not the stylist. Not me, as the owner is cutting away my hair. Vague sadnesses leak out of her. She can't find her center, she says.

But the customer is calmed by the salon. She feels comfortable, like when she is here, she can really be herself, she tells us. The way she can talk, she just can't in other places. She refers often to a surgery, and later it is clear she is talking about a breast enhancement. Before the surgery, I learn, she had a dress with a very slim fit. It looked great on her. After the surgery it didn't fit anymore. She'd bought it for $2,500, sold it for $1,500. How she phrased it, it was as though she'd made $1,500.

"No," the owner says, "you lost $1,000."

The customer more or less ignores this. She is in the salon, the place where she can be herself, where she can boast about her $1,500 profit. I understand. There is a Before and there is an After. We are in the After. Anyway, it is the stylist she comes for, not the owner. The stylist, who laughs with her, makes her hair look pretty, asks her questions, keeps the fragile momentum going.

After she leaves, the stylist starts with the remarks. It takes less than a minute – the silhouette of the departed has just barely moved across the glass window. The stylist cleans up the hair, these last parts of her, and begins disinfecting the equipment. She brings up things about the customer, who it turns out is her favorite punching bag. She starts with the surgery and then moves on to her expenditures and her attitudes. One by one, she attacks them.

"I just don't get that," she keeps saying.

If the customer had overheard, though, I would have told her not to worry about it. We all have to sell for a loss sometimes.

QUICK AND DIRTY

There is a hole in my roof, so the contractor arrives. We get into it right away. His second job could be as a professional beer drinker. His first wife, she was a cheater. He enjoys summing people up.

"You're a thinker, I can tell that."

His second wife woke up one day and decided she wanted to be somebody. She left him. The Mexicans, he complains, don't dispose of their garbage properly. Before he leaves, he tells me about his daughter, who has some disabilities. Beautiful penmanship though.

HOW ARE YOU?

I am in the kitchen, talking to my family's housekeeper. She comes every few weeks and when she does, we talk in Spanish. We laugh, we are very friendly, have been a long time. Our dog, Indy, loves her. When she comes, Indy follows her everywhere, to the kitchen, the bathrooms, even out the door, to the hallway, the laundry. She wags her tail. We talk about Indy's life sometimes, the slowness, the repetition. She sleeps, not much is ever different. The life of a dog.

I move out. Sometimes when I come back to visit, we overlap. We hug, we chat.

"How are you?" I ask.

I really want to know.

She is smiling but also not smiling.

"Always the same," she says. "Like Indy."

After her remark, I walk slowly back to my room. She seals herself away in her headphones, to fastforward through work, as I do too. The comment haunts me. So harsh, seemingly. But how serious are people during greetings anyway? Later, before she goes home, I see her petting Indy, who has rolled over in blissful submission. She is giggling. And then she is off, returning to all the parts that are different, I hope. The door closes behind her.

DETAILS

L. and I still work in the same office. Our boss doesn't know we're not together anymore, doesn't know we were ever together. He has invited us north to help with his new home and to learn about carpentry. He has been renovating for seven years, but it is finally almost finished. Every free second he has goes into the house. His Saturdays. His Sundays. His fiancée is there too; he calls her "love."

We bike past crumbling brick houses until we reach the dreamy property where they live. There is a secret passageway that joins two rooms, for their kids someday, and we squeeze through its small hole. He gives us a tour of the bedroom and the kitchen, showing us a painstaking amount of detail: seven years' worth of the texture of certain woods, of the way the light hits specific windows. It is as though his love for the house lives inside the details he describes.

L. and I are there to learn, but mostly we stand on ladders, stuffing insulation recycled from jeans. Blue dust slips past our surgical masks. It clings to our throats. One day soon, I'm sure, she will remove my picture from her wallet. We are still transitioning out of our intimacy. There is so much dust I can barely see. Not her constellation of freckles, not her ink-colored eyes.

THE HISTORY CHANNEL

My mom is friends with his mom and we hang out when we are little. Later, not so much. Years pass. His family comes to visit my family – carpets have been pulled up, walls smashed into rubble and carted away, furniture replaced or rearranged – we are grown up now. "I love The History Channel," he tells me, before even the hellos. I raise my eyebrows when he asks me if there's been anything good on lately. I tell him I have no idea and he looks hurt. I think back – it's true I used to like The History Channel when I was younger. As I'm thinking, he explains that all he heard growing up was that I watched The History Channel. "Why don't you watch The History Channel?" his mom would ask him.

IF GOD WERE A WOMAN

"Are you from around here?" a man asks me. One of those evangelical guys who seems to be a professional nuisance to the casual pedestrian.

I am heading to a cafe in the Arab Quarter of my neighborhood. We are not far from the local mosque, but this man seems to be Christian; he is holding a bible. I'm Jewish, so it feels like I'm stepping inside of a hammy joke. Like anyone else, I have been asked to stop a thousand times by someone like him and almost never have, but I happen to be in a good mood. I tell him I am in fact from around here: I live just down the block. There is a woman with him, but she doesn't speak. I am expecting to hear about Jesus, but the man would like to know if I'm aware that there is a chance God may be female. He pulls open his bible to show me a passage in Genesis with a mysterious pronoun.

"Now the earth was formless and empty, darkness was over the surface of the deep, and the Spirit of God was hovering over the waters."

It's that "spirit" that has the feminine pronoun. I'm intrigued by the idea of God as a woman and I loosen up a little bit, curious where else the conversation can go. I'm charmed by his progressive vision, and even when the talk tilts toward conversion, of what I am and am not, I start talking excitedly about a Torah I've seen recently that acknowledged some "scribal errors." I love this phrase. The idea of these scribes copying out everything by hand – the inevitable introduction of small mistakes due to the Herculean nature of their task – each version becoming its own in minor imperceptible ways that will grow over time.

"Errors?" he says.

His voice has lost some of its music. He stares at me. The woman continues to not speak, though now her silence says something.

"Thank you for sharing this with me," I say to him, but he is no longer listening.

SCREEN SAVER

"This is a big country club of nothing," complains an older white woman when she has been waiting for a few minutes in the Verizon store. A younger Black female employee is trying to figure out why my iPhone isn't charging. She's convinced that something is stuck in the slot. She pumps compressed air into it to remove lint and dust, but that doesn't work. The older woman asks if she's the manager. She is.

"The real manager?"

"The real manager."

The older woman snaps at her when she returns to my iPhone. She complains loudly to a sympathetic customer who is also waiting a few feet away from us. Her temper worsens the longer she waits. When she demands the corporate number, the employee restrains herself and simply goes to a back office and returns with it. I see her own anger flare and then retreat in her face. She is used to it, I imagine, sadly. She turns back to my iPhone, now with a thumbtack. The older woman is standing very close to us, still bitter and complaining. She is so close she sees the colored fish on my screen saver. She asks if I photographed them, full of curiosity and grandmotherly enthusiasm. I am so stunned by the shift that I just nod, even though they are illustrations from an exhibit at the Natural History Museum.

"Such nice fish," she says.

A SCREW LOOSE

I'm at the dentist, deeply reclined. She comments that my beard is new, thinking I'm my brother, until I tell her I'm not. I learn a little about her, that she likes her vacations in the three- and four-day variety, so you can have more of them.

"Not waiting for your two weeks like some dog," she says.

The dentist starts telling me about how she is still relatively new to the city – how the building jumpers are very inconsiderate when they don't wait for people to pass. She seems to think that the jumping is as New York as taxis or rats, and she worries they're going to land on her. Once she saw the aftermath in person, the police taking their time, the body still there, someone's head splattered across the sidewalk.

I'm overdue for an X-ray, so she is jockeying the machine into position, pivoting its arm. It can be contorted to support whatever position she needs, but the problem is that it won't stay still. It is moving too much on the right side. "A screw loose," she explains. Until someone fixed it, she asked patients to use their actual arm to hold the mechanical one steady above their heads while the photos are taken. She assumed the machine had the same skittishness on the left side, so she asked her patients to hold it on that side too. One of them was an engineer and he told her he didn't think that just because the mechanical arm is skittish on the right side, it will be skittish on the left. Gravity, physics, she still doesn't know exactly what, but he was right. When it held, when the mechanical arm did not quiver on the left side, "it was a blow," she tells me.

"I didn't feel well all of a sudden."

Now she wonders what other assumptions she has made.

She pulls down her surgical mask so we are face to face. In such a clinical setting, it registers almost as a kind of nudity, and my recent isolation makes the unexpected intimacy especially potent. It has such an effect on me that I consider asking her out.

How do you ask out your dentist?

She is still thinking out loud, telling me about this one moment – the screw-shaped hole in her brain.

"What other tiny errors do I make when I judge people?" she asks. "When I think about myself."

I start becoming concerned about her reliability as my dentist. She seems to spend a lot of time thinking about dead people. I like my dentists to be bland and stable. Empathetic but not too eccentric. Fixing teeth must take concentration. Consistency.

So many screws.

THE SWEETEST SHOT

We are playing three on three and he is by far the best. It seems like he never misses. He raises the ball up slowly into his stance, shoots, swish every time. He is a beautiful machine, a magic trebuchet of basketball. There is no net so the ball just goes through. I find ways to get him the ball. Bounce pass. Hand off. Down low. Guy never says a word, but we win every game. It's something I like about pickup – the instant chemistry you sometimes develop with strangers – learning each other through playing. I say goodbye and he waves. The third player, I don't even remember. I only remember the shot. My own style is awkward – I can't shoot unless I'm fading away, a runner in the lane, a tough post-up. I don't take jump shots unless I'm off-kilter, veering left so my body is a diagonal. If I miss, I can blame that. No one ever cares, but I can blame that.

Many of us who play here are afflicted by these minor basketball diseases of the brain. Someone who was told he dribbles too much so all he does is pass. Someone who is afraid to take layups, even though they are the easiest shots, since he was scorned for missing a few gimmes in a row. He'll pass backward or he'll retreat to take a much deeper shot, a Hail Mary. His stance is unusual, the ball held above his right shoulder, like a shot putter. But he does not go for layups anymore.

The same night, I'm going out to get food, I'm on my corner, I see the shooter – the shock of seeing any one stranger twice.

"Hey!"

He had such an elegant shot, I want to know what he sounds like, how he speaks, to see how far the fluency goes. The shooter turns and recognizes me, but doesn't know what to say. For the first time, the ball rattles around the rim.

"You live around here?" I ask.

"Yeah," he says, but he seems unsure how to navigate the interaction. Paralyzed almost, like he can barely speak. Or he doesn't want to, not with me.

I raise my hand in a final salute. Maybe one day we'll have a real reunion on the court.

"See you out there."

FIVE-MINUTE FRIENDSHIPS

The way this hygienist speaks is tentative at first. "Is this okay? I'm going to do this now." At the same time, her cleaning is very thorough. She likes getting rid of all the plaque, she tells me. Making people's teeth clean. The one on one of it. She doesn't mind the blood.

She notices teeth more than other people do, she thinks. Most people don't notice. We are talking about some blemishes on mine.

"I notice those," she says, "but most people wouldn't. So don't worry. I see all these women who spend fortunes on their hair, their makeup. They open their mouths and it's not good. Their breath is bad. They don't take care of their teeth."

"Have you ever noticed that?" she asks me. "People are so full of their own selves. They just don't notice."

We are not talking about teeth anymore.

"And most people don't care," I add, my teeth coated with baking soda. "Which is an antidote to self-consciousness. People don't notice you, they don't care what you do. They're in their own heads."

I am struck by this connection with the hygienist.

"It's actually freeing," I am about to say. "People worry too much. *I* worry too much."

But she speaks first. Her hands are in my mouth.

"Teeth," she says again, like it is a lyric to a catchy song.

"How can they not notice teeth?"

25

SHE USED TO BE SOMEONE ELSE TOO

It is late and the bus is still an hour away from this small town in the northern neck of upstate New York. I'm outside on a bench – inside there are pinball machines no one is playing. We start slowly. I ask if she's sure the bus will really come. "It will," she says. She sees I'm on my laptop and slips me the Wi-Fi password for the coffee shop next door. She takes out some cigarettes. On some days she has to choose, she says, cigarettes or food.

Voices come through on her walkie-talkie. Taxi drivers. She tells me how bad everything is in the town. How her taxi drivers used to be engineers. They used to be CEOs. How everyone is in decline, including her. She laughs.

One of the voices belongs to a man named Steve. He is one of the drivers. Or he is her husband.

"Bye, my love," she says to Steve.

I keep becoming invested in these little stranger interactions. I can't tell if I'm just searching for something to spice the vacant hours, or if it is because of something larger, my real life turning into a wasteland where unknowability and drama and color are flowers that no longer bloom.

"Thanks, sweetheart," she says to Steve.

I can't tell.

"Taxi driving is where they can hide," she says to me, not without sympathy. Now that they're no longer engineers, no longer CEOs.

She used to be someone else too, she tells me in between drags. Used to study anthropology. Now, she is hiding. On her days off, she says, she doesn't come here, where we are.

"Otherwise I'm just bus lady. Taxi lady."

On her days off, she doesn't want to be these things. Her walkie-talkie keeps ringing, almost every minute. When we're talking, she lets it ring longer before she presses the button to receive the call. In the parking lot, our conversation accelerates into increasingly personal territory. I tell her I think I am in decline too – she said it so I can say it. We are talking about things maybe we wouldn't talk about if we knew each other better.

"What is your name, by the way?" she asks.

The bus will be here soon, but before it comes, Steve shows up. He comes from around a corner so I can't see if he is coming from a taxi or he's just there to keep her company during the graveyard shift, to share a cigarette. I like the idea of that, of Steve speeding over for a few drags with his wife, this lonely corner a little less lonely. We all talk for a while and then Steve leaves. He heads back around the corner, and when the dispatcher starts talking about him, she still never pivots to a "we." Then she mentions an ex-girlfriend, though maybe she dates men too.

I end up appreciating the ambiguity – that all I can puzzle out of them is their fondness for each other. Then the dispatcher's walkie-talkie starts ringing again and I throw my backpack over my shoulder. As the bus pulls up, we wish each other nice lives.

ALL FIFTY STATES

I take 25 and another writer takes the other 25, but it is impossible for anyone to know who has written the entries for each state. Our bylines run under the article – not by entry. The article is called: "The Year in Weird," highlighting the strangest thing that had happened that year in every state.

A few people ask me which ones I wrote. When I talk with L., she guesses and every time she is right. Like she can tease out even the most subtle strands of self through the words.

"You wrote this one," she Gchats me.

Mark Parisi intended to 'donate' one of his testicles for $35,000 so he could purchase a Nissan 370Z, 'a serious car for serious drivers.' Parisi, something of a medical-study-for-pay addict, has taken part in an Ebola virus study and a shuttered flatlining study. He said he would have his lost testicle replaced with an artificial one.

"What tipped you off?" I ask.

"The mention of 'a serious car for serious drivers' in quotes. It's like a totally unnecessary tidbit that adds something."

I almost hope she'll get one wrong, that she never knew me as well as I thought. But I can't even hide in South Dakota.

She pastes the blurb into our text box.

The most snow the state had ever experienced was ten inches 100 years ago, but a strange blizzard brought up to four feet of snow in October. Up to 30,000 cows were feared dead, particularly vulnerable because they had not grown their winter coats yet.

"you."

THE SHEET

"Do you want to cum over?" someone texts me from a dating app that supposedly tracks people you pass in the street.

In her pictures it is a little hard to see what she looks like. But it's been a while. I call my friend to ask his advice, and also to tell him what happened, in case I should go poof.

Sure, I want to. I stop by Duane Reade, the family planning aisle, I tell her 20 minutes. While I'm walking over, she texts me again to find out how kinky I am. "Not very" is the answer, which I know she doesn't want, so I say, "How kinky are we talking about?" Quick verbal pesticide. She says whatever, just get over here already. By then I'm nearby, so I ask if we can meet at a bar, do a quick sanity check.

No.

"Ring 1F," she texts. Immediately after I step inside her building I receive a three paragraph text, too long to have been typed out right then. "The door is open," the text reads. "When you come in, you'll see a sheet on your right. The sheet has a hole in it. Put your penis through the hole."

I am standing there in the hallway. Put your penis through the hole?

I don't know what to do – I have already come all this way. I imagine being murdered, a quick knife to the gut. I imagine being robbed, the loss of my ID, my wallet, my coffee card on which I have almost attained the ten-punch prize.

The door is open, as promised. There's a sheet, as promised, and it's draped across a door frame on my right. Then I see the hole.

"Hello?" I say, like I'm in a haunted house, trying to dispel ghosts with my words.

"Put it in," a voice says.

The hole is the size of a human head. I see skin. I see curves.

"Can I see you first?" I say to whoever is behind the sheet.

Whoever is behind the sheet says no, I cannot see her first. Whoever is behind the sheet has a distinctly female voice. I imagine the knife again. I imagine having no penis. I imagine never having sex again, sheet or no sheet.

"I think I need to see you first."

"I have a boyfriend," she says.

It sounds as though she is worried one day I will see them on the street and tell him about her secret life.

"This is getting a little weird," I say from my side of the sheet. "You're not going to come out from there?"

She won't, and there is a long silence.

"Think I'm gonna go," I say at last.

"You're not kinky at all!" she yells, as I reenter the hallway and speedwalk home.

A LOVE THAT BUILDS SLOWLY

My boss and I wander uncertainly into a strip mall, hungry and lost. Neon flickers, illuminating advertisements peeling off walls. There is one place still open and they serve ice cream. We wind up sitting across from two Korean girls, 22 and 23 years old – they move over so we can sit too.

"Where are you from?"

"What are you up to?"

We are only in Los Angeles for a few days. We talk about food and they spend a long time searching on their phones, on Yelp, for places we should go. They find at least ten places and they write them all down for us.

We finish the ice cream, we are about to leave, but first I ask them about the word *jung*. I want to hear how they define it. A friend of mine told me about it once, since it's his last name. It refers to a specific type of love in Korean, he said. A love that builds slowly, that accumulates over time. I want to see what they see in the word, how they'll translate it. But I can't pronounce it so well and they think it is a different word, a near-obsolete expression of saying something's cool. I try again.

"Oh! It's kind of rural," one of the girls says. "Very hard to define, but it's about showing a kindness, an affection, even to strangers."

There is a pause. The girls feel frustrated they can't quite explain it. They haven't been able to say what they want to. Then, an epiphany. The slightly younger girl looks at me and she moves her hand back and forth between us.

"This is jung."

III

ODD LITTLE ROOMS

"Hello, Michelle," an older man says to my mom, trying to corner her in the elevator. We are 7K. He is 6K. He is the boogeyman of our building, a lumbering figure I have imagined more than I have seen. A person made out of anecdote, colored in by old details.

They have not spoken in ten years, maybe twenty – my mom won't allow it. But sometimes he ensnares her; even a lobby has narrow places. Dead ends.

"Why are you talking to me?" she says with a shudder.

•

Passenger elevators began with drama. They began with Elisha Otis standing on top of an elevator and slicing the cord. When it didn't fall, it was as though the world suddenly had permission to scrape the sky. Now, though, I associate elevators with meaningless interstitial moments. Facilitators of airless hellos no one really wants.

•

As a kid I sometimes got bored in these odd little rooms that go up and down. During rides with multiple stops, I'd study the Inspection Report Sheet like it was a secret petition, the occasional addition of a new signature, of a different inspector than the one who came before. I remember thinking about the maximum occupancy number, that even though most of the time there are just one or two people in the elevator, it is theoretically possible to jam in so many more if we are all squeezed together. It would never really happen though, could only happen in my imagination, because in reality there would barely be any room to breathe.

•

Sometimes floors are called stories. As if by sharing space, it is inevitable that we will share other things too.

•

I am in the elevator with a boy and his mom. He is slashing a key against the two strips of silver that run vertically down the wall, where there are already star shaped scratches. His mom tells him to stop and she gives me a look like, "He's a handful."

If anyone had looked closely, they would have seen a *JS* among the scratches, but no one ever has – no one has done this simple math. I have kept the secret for a long time. When I was younger, I was known for scrupulously following rules, but in this room for some reason I was liberated. For some reason it was okay to be someone else.

I take out my key and point to the scratches.

"That was me when I was a kid," I confess.

For a second the concerned mom is shocked and then she bursts out laughing.

•

"Why are you talking to me?" my mom says to the

boogeyman. "I can't talk to you. After what you did to me and my family? Don't come near me. Please."

But he tries again, and then again.

If she says hello back, then it will be like it didn't happen. So she won't say it – she will not say hello.

When I was six years old, I devoted every idle moment to basketball. I had a hoop in my room and I dribbled with a Nerf ball, pretending I was my favorite players. I was the offense and then I was the defense. 6K heard the noise sometimes and complained. He lived alone, rarely went out. My mom tried to get me to stop, but basketball was what I loved. She bought a soft padding for the floor to absorb the sound. Not enough.

•

Years later, when I tell the story of what happened, I tell everyone he had a dog. A big dog. This is what I remember, but my mom says there was no dog.

My brother had just been born – he was still waking up in the middle of the night, so my mom woke up, too. It was four in the morning. She heard something and opened the front door. She saw someone running down the stairs – a bit of a person. She couldn't follow him, because she was holding my brother, but she was sure it was 6K.

From the knob to the top lock, our door was smeared in shit.

My mom called the police. She was so upset she forgot it was evidence, put down my brother and desperately tried to scrub it away. The surreal fact remained: someone had saved it up, perhaps in jars.

Just from talking to 6K, the police said they could tell it was him, but there was no hard proof. Still, he was fully dressed – my mom remembers the police saying that to her.

"Who's fully dressed at 4:30 in the morning?"

•

A dog – the only way a child could make sense of it. Or maybe a clever fairy tale my mom invented the next day. We are talking about it now, two decades later. I am trying to get my mom to see his side of things, how much it must have bothered him, all the dribbling. His one refuge, the apartment, under attack.

•

When I was a teenager, I just knew him to be the building boogeyman, the story my mom told. The one or two times I saw him he looked as though a real emotion had never passed through his face. The way my mom spoke about the boogeyman, I stared him down in the elevator. I even smashed my shoulder into him on the way out once, feigning a sense of rush, battling through the crowd of one. I wonder if he has any idea who I am. I wonder if I am becoming the villain.

•

"It was so many years ago," 6K says to my mom when she can't escape. He does not define "it."

"Are you actually talking to me?" my mom asks.

•

When I'm younger, there is a different older man I talk

to in the elevator. He likes the Giants and I like the Jets, so every ride is loud with amusing taunts fresh from the latest games. Then I'm in the elevator and I'm older; it is tougher for him to tease, his voice hoarse, something drained from him. One day I'm in the elevator and he is stooped, his still-bright Giants windbreaker almost like a tarp over his shrunken body. There is silence as the floor numbers tick upward. He doesn't even notice me anymore.

•

I wonder if infrequency is more revealing than frequency. If we are so close sometimes we can't see anything at all.

•

Thirteenth floors are considered unlucky, so sometimes they are skipped. The building where I grew up stops at 13 – instead it is called PH for penthouse. Theoretically, you can see more from the roof. An aerial view.

For the first time in years, I run into the boogeyman. I come back to visit sometimes and there he is. His walk is slow and awkward, his joints hardened. A Frankenstein. I am conscious of myself as younger and faster.

I decide I'll hold the door for him – this prisoner in the holding cell of my imagination. I can't resist the possibility of confrontation, of seeing him up close. I stare. His face has a spectral quality, an eerie gray. His skin is a roll of unwashed human carpet.

All of my perspective, my sense of distance – so quickly it reaches its vanishing point. I think of my mom, of twenty years ago, and I feel myself boiling over. The elevator ascends and I don't know yet what I will say.

What nastiness is within.

But before I can become me, he speaks. I am just someone who held a door, it turns out. He is just someone trying to get home.

"Thanks," he says.

IV

IS THAT YOU?

"Some people will scream when they see a mouse run across the floor. Other people go out in the forest and chase a bear around. I've actually touched the eels. It's not as big of a jolt as a spark plug on a running engine, but it's more constant."

"You work at the aquarium?"

"I volunteer. I'm in between jobs and it's something to do. I've done a lot of stuff there's no record of me doing. I can assist you in surgery if you need it. You want to see the tape? Most of my friends don't like watching this. This is the guy's right hip. I'll show you something only three people in here know. At one time I was the most well-known naturalist photographer in Michigan. I'd exhibit in galleries. I'd sit on a waterfall all day long and take one picture."

"You took those?"

"Yes. I don't belong here, okay? I've processed more than a million rolls of Kodak film. I make IV fluid for humans. You saw me in the operating room. If I wasn't driving my uncle around to all his doctor

appointments and my dad wasn't sick, if my mother hadn't just passed away, I'd be somewhere makin' money. You know what I mean?"

STREETBALL

I'm fighting with someone for a loose ball and we get tangled up. "Jump," I say. "Jump ball." A player on the other team scoffs.

"There are no jump balls in streetball," he says.

He's been calling fouls on me the whole game and now this, so I get even more aggressive. Defense is when I can really be myself, when I can hurl my body with abandon, when I don't have to worry about making mistakes. It seems like people think I'm sweet. Like sometimes that's all they see. "You're too nice," people say to me. My preferred self-image comes from the stapled and long-faded pages of my old summer camp sports newspaper, where someone once characterized me as "a fiery guard with a mean streak." Even if there were only a fistful of copies of surely one of the world's least read periodicals, this is how I see myself.

I haven't played pickup basketball in a long time, but I am here. For my job working remotely, I just type in bed, sometimes for so long, I feel like Charlie's idle grandfather from *Willy Wonka & the Chocolate Factory*. Hardening into human furniture. But now I am here.

Lighters fall out of pockets. Tiny candies scatter over the cement. None of us knows each other: we have to discover each other's rhythms, study tendencies, anticipate cuts and drives and shots. On the high walls of the fence are four plastic sculptures, yellow banisters pretzeled into people. They loom above us, always there, always playing, their faces circles. Often when I play, I am just the color of my shirt.

"Pass it, blue."

"Don't shoot that, red."

It's a vacation from all the rest of it, when I have to be more than a color.

I'm still guarding the same guy. He's dribbling and I take the ball away. I steal it. He starts whining that I reached in, that I fouled him again. He is so angry, some of the other players have to hold him back. He's threatening me and I can see across the free throw line that he is starting to tear up.

"There is no crying in streetball."

THE CORPORATE LADDER

"Where do you want to be in five years?" a prospective employer asks me. I have flown halfway across the country for this interview on my own dime. An email said they were "intrigued by my unorthodox background," and they're already an unorthodox company, so I'm not as concerned about presenting my most corporate self. I am trying to explain my concept of horizontal ambition, that there's nowhere I really want to get to but there's a lot I want to do — it is not going so well.

"What's wrong with ambition?" the man asks at the other end of the conference table.

Two things are clear: a beautiful view of the Hudson River and how much I have miscalculated.

"You know, like Macbeth."

MR. REJECTION

"Let's scroll ahead – this is too depressing," says the chuckling 42-year-old, an engineer and a prolific inventor of things that never made it to market. As part of a quirky lecture series in a remodeled warehouse, the speaker is presenting a life's worth of his personal, professional, and romantic failures.

When someone asks what lasting lesson he's learned from failed products like the heel slide – a revolutionary advancement over the shoehorn – he replies that he makes sure now to send a self-addressed stamped envelope along with his applications to ensure he'll get something in writing rather than email. It's more dramatic that way, he says wistfully, as if the good old days are long gone. The audience erupts in laughter. He references a project about how animal sounds differ by culture.

"Somehow film festivals weren't interested in that," he deadpans.

The presenter seems to revel in the harshest responses he's collected over the years. Committee Member Two of the 2007 Cleveland International Film Festival, for instance, did not like his documentary *Driving in India*:

"Having experienced what the film discussed," the reviewer says, "I expected a more serious take on it. Instead I found it to be dull with a monotone narration, bland statistics, and uninteresting visuals. Even at 38 minutes long, I was surprised that it dragged."

The monotone narration?

"That was me," the speaker assures the audience.

After the presentation is over, there is a brief Q & A.

"Where does the money come from?" a drunk guy barks at the speaker.

"I work on the Tappan Zee Bridge."

There is total silence. It seems like the audience thinks he spends his days in a tollbooth collecting singles and fives. Maybe all this failure he's described isn't so funny or performative – maybe it's real.

"Whoa! That put a hush on the crowd. What's the problem with that? I'm a structural engineer. What's wrong with that? Bridges. Tunnels," he says and the audience slowly resuscitates through scattered laughter.

DADDY

What he wants is against the editorial policy, but he doesn't care. I've written a profile of someone who's demanding to read it before it's published. It is almost always a bad idea. I say no but he checkmates me with a shrewd ultimatum: he won't agree to meet with the photographer unless I send it to him. My subject calls back later to tell me he loves it. There is just one thing. He showed it to his daughter and she saw all his swear words. He wants them taken out. Deleted. He has a hard time believing he used those words. I have the recording, though. His daughter thinks I must've gotten it wrong too.

"Daddy, you don't curse like that," she told him over the phone.

THE THREE NEWSPAPERS

It's true: growing up we have three different newspapers delivered. Three different versions of the world: *The Times*, *The Post*, *The Journal*. They are read, folded, and abandoned throughout our apartment. I am speaking with my dad's associate on the phone and he mentions the three newspapers like it is a keystone fact about my dad. Three newspapers a day. A peculiar but admirable diet. It has never occurred to me before to see it this way, to even think about it. I only really read one of them – for the sports. I've never needed a shorthand for understanding my dad: he's my dad. Or maybe this is a form of myopia, of psychological trimming, of not forcing ourselves to reimagine who people are because we think we already know them. By the time I meet this man who once worked with my dad, he continues to mention the three newspapers. My dad is like anyone else, he scans the paper, he reads what interests him, but if you ask the associate, my dad doesn't miss a sentence, not one.

A SINGLE WORD

At a small magazine, I get to work with an accomplished writer. I prefer to be behind the scenes, editing rather than reporting, and he teases me for how much I like to be in the background.

"White on white, huh?" he says about my idea for a new project and we laugh.

"There's too much of you in this piece," I'll say sometimes, when I'm the writer's editor.

He jokes that I always want to cut him out, but as a person, I try to spend as much time with him as I can. He lends me clothes so I can sneak into his tennis club, teaches me how to jab with his old gloves, tears down my writing so he can build it back up. I put in late hours, weigh in on his romantic dilemmas, iron out snarls in his longform. Almost a year after I meet him, I decide I'll read his nonfiction book. He is a character in it, a reporter hot on the trail of a puzzling case, but it's hard to recognize him. Not that the him in the book is a virtuoso acting performance but it is just a little different from the person I have come to know. I admire how much of himself he's kept out, to let the story just be the story, but I can't help feeling a sense of distance, like maybe I don't know him so well after all.

Something I like about him is how inventive he is with language. One time I call him up and he asks how I'm doing.

"Just trying to come up for air," I say.

"I didn't know there was any left," he says. "Can

you bottle some up for me?"

He refers to the stories I work on as "my end of the empire."

I hold onto his phrases like they're souvenirs.

The way I hit the Ping-Pong ball, he says it moves like a "drunken mosquito." Sometimes I tell people that's my nickname.

Toward the end of the book, I run into the word "cannibalize." I've seen it in his stories before and it always seems like he uses it in an awkward way, meaning to convert the remains of one thing into something else. As in, the seamstress cannibalized an old raincoat to make a scarf. He relies on it a lot, and I usually try to remove it, distracted by the image of humans eating other humans instead of a basic sentence about a raincoat, or another inanimate object.

When I'm first reading his book I feel like just another reader, but then there it is, that one word I know. I'm glad to trip over it this time. All of a sudden I feel inside, in the ink. I know this man.

THE RIGHT COMBINATION

For years one of the dads refers to my brother as the gnat. It's not a private nickname. He says it in front of him. The gnat. Always around, annoying.

"Go away, gnat."

"What do you want, gnat?"

When my brother is a teenager, he has some trouble and the people where we spend our summers don't really understand him. He's at an age that makes him too young for my friends, but too old for their siblings. This dad – his son is kinder. His son is my friend. When this friend dies in a tragic accident, my brother will grieve too.

"He's the only one who was ever nice to me."

During these summers, my brother always feels excluded; all he wants is to be around. To be the gnat. But he is always shooed away. This friend lets him stay when we're all hanging out even more than I do. My little brother who wears a necklace with the letters of his name printed on small silver cubes: E-V-A-N. Somehow the letters always get jumbled and never align into the right combination. This friend has a nickname for him too, but it doesn't involve insects. He calls my brother Neva, since that's the word the letters often form. N-E-V-A. It becomes a badge of affection. Thinking about it now, I appreciate it even more. Like how people saw my brother was just lost in translation.

THE THINGS THAT FALL BETWEEN

He was telling me about a girl he'd met. Now they've been together a long time, but then he barely knew her. They were splayed across his couch – it was the first time they kissed. One of her earrings fell off, slipped into the crevice between the cushions. They couldn't find it, but after she left he was able to extract the earring. He decided not to tell her, to keep it, a memento of their night, one where there might not be another. In fact, he never told her, perhaps concerned the evening had not appreciated in value for her the way it had for him.

I think about this sometimes, the things that fall between, the fragments of people we keep that they may not remember. For me, these things have most often been words, phrases, things I've said. Someone I bumped into on the street remembered a young version of me running over to him in first grade screaming, "I'm going to have a brother!" I was in awe of such an earnest version of myself, so grateful to rediscover, or even learn about him on a walk back from the East River. Recently, someone else remembered the way I picked apart a vacation he went on in high school. He'd gone to the beach, bicycled through the town. "That's all you did?" he said I said. What was just a passing comment to me, a thoughtless remark, lodged in him for almost a decade. That it was really me who prodded him like that I initially denied and protested, but I was forced to admit I knew this version too.

It makes me wonder which other of my selves are

walking around this city, strangers even to each other. It is odd what slips through in comfort, what stays in the deep cushions. But if someday an old aspect is shown to you, you still might recognize it, even if time has turned it foreign, even if you have to hold your earring up to the light.

THE VOLUME WAS LOW

I'm in L.'s city, so we agree to meet for lunch. After the lunch, we won't speak for eight months. We each order waffles, but both of us are slow eaters and there is not much time. I am telling her about my night – some things we shouldn't talk about – so I am telling her about my night. I watched a movie with an old buddy of mine. Weeks ago, instead of texting me about other things, she texted me about the same movie. How much she liked it.

As we are picking at the waffles, I tell her that I didn't like it so much. The movie. Wasn't sure how I felt about it.

She looks up at me.

"I don't know you anymore," she says.

At first I think she is half-kidding and she is. But I can also hear something else in it, an echo of something she's told herself before. That phrase. The movie is for her a small confirmation.

I am just trying to say I don't love a movie, but I am already making excuses.

"I could barely hear it," I say.

My friend's roommates came home and they were talking. They wouldn't shut up. I had to strain to hear, I tell her. The volume was low. It wouldn't go any higher.

THE PERSON WHO WILL
CHANGE YOUR LIFE

She's a week early. I'm a minute late. We've both botched purchasing our bus tickets, so we have to get new ones. We'd been in the front of the line, but now we're at the back. We're in it together. She looks younger than me, maybe it's her backpack, but as we're talking, she says something about people "our age." She's going to her friend's wedding soon – I tell her one of my friends already has a divorce under his belt. Within the first minute or so, it comes out that her brother has a "baby mama," which is a separator between us, at least in my mind. That phrase isn't in my active vocabulary. When you first meet someone, details about them seem especially rich with meaning, helping you make the subtle calculations and adjustments that turn a stranger into someone you know.

We chat as the line shrinks toward the bus. She lives in the 60's all the way west, an actress. I grew up in the 60's all the way east, a writer. I'd rather sit alone since I always seem to have productive writing sessions on buses. At the exact moment I begin wading through the aisle, a guy leaves to sit with his friend and a window seat opens up. I dart into the row. Meanwhile, the girl from the line is one seat ahead of me but doesn't see me. Then she does.

"Is anyone sitting with you?"

My backpack is propped up next to me, code for *Stay Out*.

"Do you mind if I sit with you?"

She's audibly relieved when I nod yes. I take out my laptop after a bit, but she asks me something and it starts. She tells me about her interest in photography, her struggles as an actress, and then somehow we're talking about her suicidal ideations, how there was one time she was really going to do it.

Her disclosure unnerves me. Half-seen landscapes slip away through the big glass windows. Long bus trips sometimes feel like an oblivion, uprooting passengers from the landmarks of time and place. Without them, an intense conversation – especially one in such close proximity – becomes a setting in itself. Just by sitting there, I'm pulled deeper into her riptide. She tells me about a screenplay she's working on about someone who was dying and someone who wanted to die. She says she'd been both, had basically grown up in a hospital. As we speak, she keeps mentioning how sometimes someone will change your life, but there's no way to know who it is. I hope she isn't hoping it's me. She has already gotten excited because my birthday is her half birthday – an "un-birthday" in her words, which she says is six months away from your birthday. To me, an un-birthday sounds like the day you die.

Lately, many directors have been turning her down. They say, "You're actually incredible, but I can't use you." She asks them to just tell her the truth.

"That is the truth," they say.

She wants to take pictures of people's faces, headshots as emotional studies. People with mental illness. "There's a stigma on them," she says, and she wants to do her best to show that there shouldn't be.

It's a door: I tell her about the depression I've gone through. We are on a bus full of people, but I don't want her to feel alone. She Facebook friends me when I'm right next to her.

"Would you mind?"

I'd assumed she was so undisguised in what she told me earlier because I was a transient bus person she'd likely never see again, but her request complicates that belief. She seems to have no trace of my cynicism toward the value and weight of a Facebook friendship – I see that she's sincerely trying to connect with me, and I'm moved by the gesture.

Later, the bus arrives and we take a last ride together on the 1 train. I know we probably won't see each other again, and there isn't much left to say. She says thank you. Thank you for making the time pass so much faster. I thank her too.

I'm not the person who will change her life, but so what? I tell her about an inexpensive photography workshop I know, because she keeps mentioning cameras and she doesn't seem to know how to use them. She calls the buttons dials and says she'll flip them. I tell her about *Harold & Maude*, which is about death, like her screenplay. I tell her I'm looking forward to seeing her movie in theaters.

CROWDS

A whale scientist is describing to us the bloody mess of whale autopsies. She has to wear chain mail and gloves, because the insides of whales are so slippery the knife could easily cut her. This podcast taping is the first time I am meeting the friends of a new person I'm dating. It's been going well and I feel like maybe I'm finally moving on from L.

We're sitting at the bar, the stage perpendicular to our left. I am one seat to the right of her, one seat farther from the stage. Sometimes, she looks back at me to see if I am enjoying the show. The researcher starts talking about whale burials, about the difficulties of whale transportation in death – so difficult that many are buried deep in beaches beyond the tide line. She says this like it is a fact, but to me it sounds unbelievable. There is a group, she says, The Concerned Peoples of The Whales, that keeps silent guard over these graveyards. They alone know where the whales are buried. She seems to be saying that almost every beach has a hidden whale somewhere beneath it. I am tracing over my date's back with my fingers, so she knows how happy I am just to sit next to her. All her friends are to the left, they are ahead, so I feel comfortable with this affection, that it is not too much, that the only people who will see are people I don't know. Being in a crowd is a veil of privacy. To them, I am just guy and she is just girl.

A little later, a few days, she is Gchatting with an ex-boyfriend. He is still interested in her – he wants to rekindle things, he says. She tells him that she is seeing someone.

"I know," he says.

He saw the whole choreography of my private affection. He sat there and watched it. He heard about the whales too.

WHICH WORLD WE'RE IN

I only really go when I'm down, when there's little else. When what I need right then is to be just black, to be just blue. When I am walking to the court, from the angle on the street corner, I can see only the two hoops through the fences. Nothing below, just the rings of iron. It is the same every time: I don't see the basketballs, just the hoops, and I think maybe no one is there, maybe there will be no one to play with. But as I get closer, as I wait, there they are, still no hands, no bodies, but the ball fires upward as if by a cannon, one and later another – this is the sequence, this is how it goes.

There are just three guys on one of the courts. I start shooting on the one next to them. After I put my keys down, I see him. The guy, who months before seemed to loathe me – who told me there's no jump ball in streetball. I am pretty sure it's him; he keeps staring at me. Every few seconds, it seems. Maybe he remembers what I said to him and he has just been biding his time. Maybe he sees that I am all alone.

Or maybe he just wants to see what's going on, is simply looking because I am all there is to look at right then. Maybe he is hoping for a fourth player so they can run two on two.

I don't know which of the two worlds we're living in and I can't focus until I find out. I ask if they want to play, to will the world I want into reality. Or at least to get the other one to reveal itself. It turns out their fourth is coming; he is right over there parking the car.

But we can squeeze in a quick game first, they say.

I'm thinking I'll be on his team, and it'll be a re-shuffling. We'll win, high-five, be our own Stockton and Malone. Later we'll laugh about the jump ball. But I am not picked for his team. He's guarding me. I'm guarding him. Again. We are right back where we were.

In these games and in this one especially, it strikes me how error-prone we all are at keeping score. After every few points, if there's not one person who is the de facto scorekeeper, someone tries to remember. Each time it is this new remembering. 12-7 becomes 11-8. 16-14 becomes 17-13. The score is the story of the game and we are constantly getting it wrong. Sometimes, it works out, if a team gives themselves an extra point, someone will subtract a point a while later, karma of the basketball court. But often, it's just wrong, and we all accept this new reality. We just play on. As my man goes up for a shot, my hands are up high.

"Nice defense," he says.

Later, he makes a jumper.

"Nice take," I say.

After a while, he's anyone else and so am I. I still don't know for sure that it is him, if he too has traced the zigs and zags of such a small history. All I know is that each game is its own.

V

THE MAN WHO HAS EVERYTHING

When Riley[1] was nine years old, his uncle offered him a deal: for every minute he stood in freezing cold seawater he could earn one dollar. Little Riley shivered his way to sixty bucks. We are looping around the slot machines as he unfurls this legend of himself. All these years later as Dr. John's sound engineer, Riley says his salary is $500,000. One of many anecdotes, the seawater story reminds me of the way a tycoon might recall his exact starting salary as if it were some kind of scar. $500,000 I calculate afterward, in lieu of other things I can't figure out about him, is nearly a year's worth of standing in that cold water.

"It's you! It's you!" a turbaned woman says, pointing at Riley and staring in disbelief as we walk down the winding staircase to the casino.

Riley is this guy who everyone seems to know. Or at least, recognize. People share a laugh with him in the casino and they gape at him when we walk through downtown St. Louis. These sightings happen frequently even in the one day that I spend with him, like he is somehow a celebrity of anonymity. He looks blankly at the turbaned woman for several seconds before she jogs his memory with an anecdote involving an underage girl, a

---

1 Riley is a pseudonym.

creepy older man, and horse racing. That is enough for Riley, who remembers stories but not people. His lack of recognition is pervasive, a legacy he chalks up to years of snorting cocaine. He tries to live to the hilt: the word *winning* tattooed across his right wrist, the overgrown tail of the "g" flatlining under the rest of the word. Though the cocaine has stopped, he tells me, since the birth of his son Aidan, who is now two.

When I hear he has a son, I take a step back, my image of him radically changing with each new piece of information. He looks barely 25. I've only known him for about an hour: I got off the train right at the edge of St. Louis, next to the Arch, and he was just someone else walking down the steps. He complained aloud about a homeless man who begged for his cigarettes, but then he offered one to me. I decided to take the cigarette – he could be who I'm looking for. He warns me in advance, though, of I don't know exactly what.

"I'm like an 18-wheeler," he says, chuckling to himself. "I'll run you over."

We scrape away the usual veneers of introductory conversation: all of a sudden he is in a hotel in New Zealand and there's a couple on their honeymoon. He courts the wife, sleeps with her, all before the newly minted husband figures it out. They come to blows in the lobby and then the husband is on the ground. Riley seems surreal, a character from a story: his name is an alias, his legal one a skin he's shed, except to those who know him best. I feel a listener's high, escaped from my routines. There is nothing he won't tell me.

Sometimes he needs a break, he says in his raspy voice. In between tour dates, he is a regular at Casino Queen, the lowliest of the casinos in an area known topographically as the American Bottom. I tell Riley I've never been, hoping he will offer himself as my guide. His 80-cents-a-pack Smoker's Choice cigarette is about to burn out, but he agrees to take me.

We are surrounded by casinos. The Lumiere is to our west, and right next to it, there used to be a riverboat called *The President*, he says. I'm skeptical – how could there be so many so close together? Maybe this guy just talks a big game. Then Riley makes a seemingly random detour to an old lamppost, pries open what looks like a secret compartment at its base and pulls out a long roll of tickets stamped with *The President's* name. He holds it in his hands like it is the intestines of a sacred animal, gives me one and keeps none for himself.

After we run into the turbaned woman, she calls his hero, Charlie Sheen, retarded.

"Retarded and rich," Riley corrects.

She rolls her eyes after everything he says, at once aghast and half-chuckling.

A self-described redneck from Alabama, he dropped out of college and then got married at Navy Pier in Chicago. He is around five foot six with a small gauge in his left ear, black with a skeleton on it, a contrast to his pale skin. Our train rattles away from the Arch into downtrodden East St. Louis, which is in Illinois, on the other side of the Mississippi – it is so easy here to move from one state to another.

"Someday even your dick gonna get limp," the turbaned woman says.

"I'm gonna be young forever," Riley parries.

I wonder about him – about how much you can know about someone just by observing them. His hands have the pallor of an old baseball mitt, like they won't come clean. The drug use is maybe not so surprising in the life of a musician on tour, the intense stimulation and then idle nothingness, but it must be challenging – Riley's corroded memory makes everyone a potential stranger or a dear friend. He seemingly can only identify a person through their reactions to him, so in his mind, these statuses seem to be always in flux. He tells me that he has little to do with his family, his parents divorced since he was three. He is out of touch with his brother and sister.

"After a while," he says, "they're just some other people."

A dazed older woman drifts past us across a desert of parking lot. We walk toward the casino's façade, with its big golden mirrors reflecting scrawls of the highway that slices through East St. Louis. We are on the very edge – casino guests never really go inside the city. East St. Louis was once a thriving corporate suburb that doubled in the 1950's as a prominent cultural center. Now St. Louis equates its eastern brother with death. A single minute in No Man's Land and you'll be gunned down, people say in racialized whispers. But you also hear about a core of residents who stayed loyal to their community through all the hard years. That really, you're more likely to hear crickets than gunshots. It is hard to know quite what to believe when all you have are anecdotes. The city is full of stories that read like myths: "rats as big as puppies" running across the streets, according to one book on the area. It is odd to finally be in this city I have heard so much about and at the same time, to not really be in it at all.

Riley banters his way past the security guards, avoiding the ID check that is mandatory for every guest. Security is otherwise tight: vans patrol, dozens of lights guarantee that the area never darkens, and the parking lot serves as a buffer from the city proper.

I follow Riley through the elderly populations of Albert Pujols fans. I'm a hungry depository for his monologues – he never asks anything about me. He is jerky and hurried, constantly itching, trembling, unable to stay in one place, a contrast to the hunkered others, knees shackled against the machines, hands propped against their jowls, oozing up loose flesh. I am lost and disoriented, colored lights flashing across the ceiling like false North stars, but he knows exactly where he is going. He is showing me around like the casino is his private manor, and the employees his butlers.

"I love you, Susan," he calls out to an older redhead, before whispering to me that she is the worst dealer in the place. There was a time he was cursing at her and she yelled at him. He yelled back and flung a nickel at her face, without repercussion. If she breaks out of her role in any way, showing how she really feels about him or seeking revenge, he can just fill out a feedback form, file a flurry of complaints.

"She has to be nice to me," he explains.

There is an esoteric sign near the bathroom, where I run to get down the notes of our conversation. I originally went down to the river because I needed to profile someone for a writing workshop – I had an idea about talking to fishermen about odd things the Mississippi tided in, but before I could even search, there was Riley, for some reason looking for me. That sense of providence permeated the whole day, like the river offered him up instead. Just a few months earlier, I was too shy to interview someone for an assignment, so I talked to my uncle instead. And now, here is Riley with outstretched arms. The sign on the door displays an off-balance stick figure, a warning that the bathrooms are often slippery, and indeed they are inexplicably waterlogged, like the Mississippi might be leaking in. The casino exploited a loophole in the law that said Illinois citizens could only gamble on boats. Taking advantage of a legal fiction, the original boat was decommissioned and replaced by an actual building, normal except for its vast underground trench of water. Casino Queen – which resembles a wan yellow McMansion – floats on 340,000 unseen gallons.

The colored lights of the slot machines flow like liquid candy. The dozens of black eye in the sky cameras look like they're about to drip from the ceiling. Even the cleavage of the staff are lathered in sparkles. "I wish *I* could get her wet," Riley says when a waitress spills a drink.

In the glutted local casino market, Casino Queen occupies an especially cheap niche, where, with its one-dollar minimum bets, anyone can gamble. "The Home of the Loosest Slots," its billing goes. But Riley heralds the maraschino cherries as if they have been gathered from some obscure garden in the Far East. He refers to the free sodas like they are fabulous cocktails.

"If I were ever homeless, I would come live here," Riley says.

Whenever he throws down one of his cigarette butts, he stomps on it mercilessly, extinguishing any last flicker of life. He does this specifically so that the homeless can't pick it up and smoke the remains. He keeps alluding to hypothetically living on the street, but he hates homeless people. So much so that I briefly wonder if he is homeless himself. For a time in Chicago, he says, he even switched from cigarettes to chewing tobacco, so no one would approach him on the sidewalk. In the casino though, he can talk to anyone.

"Twanya! Twanya! Twanya!" he calls out in one of his flirtatious conversational love affairs, even when Twanya, a dealer, is out of earshot. She is already shaking her head when he sits down at her roulette table, trying not to laugh, each of their interactions slightly differing versions of the same strange play.

"She does have a nice smile," a guy at the table says, paying tribute to Riley's infatuation. Later Riley says he'd die to get with Twanya. Other times he says it's all a game, all a joke, and he is nothing if not loyal to his fiancée, Haley.

During one of his smoking breaks, Riley goes out of his way to befriend two Black women: he sings off-key songs to them in accompaniment to a spasmodic dance, discussing history and making them laugh, predicting that if he were at the new World Trade Center Memorial in New York, he'd probably fall into the memory pools he'd be so drunk. He talks about "history" like it is a tangible thing, a Grecian urn that can break if you drop it.

"You guys have so much history," he says.

Though I know him to be somewhat racist, that facet of him temporarily disappears. He says to me that he's not really racist, that it is just performance, that later when we are talking about koi fish and he proclaims that the whites are worth more because they're higher class and he's sorry that human whites aren't that way anymore, he's just kidding. He certainly doesn't mention to the women the mind-boggling discovery when he was younger, when he was looking through his attic and found photographs of his great-grandfather dressed in the pointed white hood of the Ku Klux Klan. He doesn't mention that his wife Haley's family is the Vanderhoff family, supposedly responsible for a significant portion of the slave trade to the British colonies. Turns out, before he was seven years old, he'd never even seen a Black person.

Instead, he talks about his admiration for Martin Luther King, Jr., and it is obvious the women like him. One of them has seen him before and recalls his quest to obtain the flag that flew on the scrapped casino riverboat, *The Admiral*. Riley has good news – he finally got it, putting a call in to the casino's CEO. She never doubts him. Some day, he says, it's gonna be worth big money. Though he told me earlier that the flag is in pristine condition, he admits now that it is a little ripped.

Maybe the rip gives it character – maybe it shows that it's real, I think.

"I'm so glad you got that flag," the woman says.

I am continually jarred by this man and recoil at certain aspects of his personality, but something else starts to happen too. Spend enough time with anyone and you begin to find a few acres of common ground. Even though we are in a place where *winning* means jackpots, the way he speaks about the word tattooed on his wrist seems to transcend dollars and cents.

I tell him about a time I was scooping out stones from a mountain spring and pulled up a diamond ring, sparkling in the sun. In awe of the ring as much as my luck, I hustled down the slope, diamond clenched in my fist. It turned out to be cracked and nearly worthless, but the rapture of the moment has always stayed with me. My heart raced. My body became light. I trembled in the water.

"Winning! That's winning!" he says with a shriek, as if he had been speaking a foreign language and is at last understood.

Riley's biggest win came with a stroke of luck, which may be the reason he is so drawn to casinos. He stumbled into the lucrative sound engineering gig after he was in the right place at the right time, in a bar when the old engineer had bailed. Now, Riley's left wrist is tattooed with his boss's name. When not on tour, he guards his phone jealously – his sole linkage to the band when he is not with them. "If I lose it, I'm fired," he says. It

sounds like he's gotten to know Dr. John – Mac Reben-
nack when he's not on stage – quite well, describing him
in detail, like how he'd gotten part of his ring finger
blown off – small facts that are part of multi-chapter
anecdotes. Riley is still mourning the death of one of the
band members, who died of cancer. Talking about it, he
is almost moved to tears.

His life has improved since he joined. He has his
own taxi driver on retainer and a team of talented law-
yers always on his side to smooth over his frequent bar
scuffles. For all his obsessions and preoccupations with
money, he knows it only goes so far, that there are things
that no amount can buy. For Dr. John's birthday, Riley
wasn't sure what to get his boss.

"What do you get a man who has everything?"

So he sent him a check for a penny, he tells me as
we walk around and around Crazy Cash Mystery Jackpots and Stinkin' Rich and Life of Luxury, under little
tubes of light, plastic veins illumined in red and green.
The main room is a little larger than a football field, with
roulette and black jack tables surrounded by clusters of
slot machines, cartoonish grinning cowboys, exaggerated
ethnic stereotypes, oversized teeth, the exoticized eyes of
Cleopatra. Sports cars and gold bricks scroll across the
screens. The vending machines are stuffed with Exce-
drin, Motrin, Alka Seltzer and Advil. Signs wonder if you
are "Spinning Out of Control?"

"Out of luck?"

I have no idea where Riley has been or who he really is, but I can tell he feels right at home. I keep thinking about his cigarette. The *Smoker's Choice*, the cheap
paper. And his allotment for the casino: a pocketful of
quarters from his wife. I remember his supposed large
salary.

"I slip," Riley says, when I press him on some of the small inconsistencies, like how he refers to his wife Haley alternatively as girlfriend and fiancée. Still, he offers to introduce me. He met her at age five and they have dated since the eighth grade. He justifies his extra-marital affairs by saying that if a person doesn't know something, that something might as well not exist. He says this as if lies are just games of perspective, small surgeries we all perform to make the world as we want it to be. I don't agree but find myself fascinated by how he moves through the world, so casual with the truth, turning everything into a laugh, slavishly committed to carpe diem. Our impromptu cross-state gallop lasts eight hours.

Maybe it is all the fresh oxygen pumped into the casino air, the strategic lack of clocks, or the unlikelihood of our connection, but I feel unusually locked into the present tense, hanging on every word. I've never met anyone quite like him. So open and raw.

"I'm as real as you get," he told me when we first met. "I won't sugar-brush nuthin.'"

In a way, I was the less honest one: I tell Riley all the texting I am doing is with L., inventing a dispute that must be constantly attended to. The truth is that I am texting myself the notes of our conversation so I can write it later for the workshop – as a self-taught cub writer, I don't yet know I should state my purpose up front. The truth is also that we manage to have a good time. Almost as an afterthought, I give him my phone number at the end of the night.

•

Two days later, he calls. If I had picked up the first time he called, maybe it would have been different, but I don't pick up because I am on a walking tour of an old neighborhood. He calls again. And again. He calls 14 times over a span of three days because he wants to go back to the casino. The Queen. He wants to relive the day we had, the day we talked and talked.

Fourteen times. I become worried that I'm at the core of some scheme, the way he lit up when I told him that I attended a private university. I see that he's sipped my attention and wants more. I barely know Riley – all I know is what he told me. Like when he told me about escalating a bar room brawl. He went outside to his adversary's brand new Corvette, slashed the tires, slid across the hood and punched in the windows. The Corvette owner lay in a crumpled drunken heap watching the destruction. Riley offered the man his business card as a stylized Fuck You. There is an underlying violence to him that I find terrifying. When the Corvette story is finished, Riley shows me his hands. He shows me the scars.

He told me how a *Riverfront Times* reporter wrote an unflattering profile of him – Riley framed it on his wall, but if he ever got his hands on the reporter now, he said, he'd beat the hell out of him.

I stare at my phone, and for a moment, I wonder what it would've been like if our roles were reversed, if Riley had followed me around – what judgments he would've made and what truths he would have found within the flimsy structure of a single day, limited to so few flecks of context. But then I wonder about the fighting and his fixation on money. I am scared that he wants something – it never occurs to me that maybe he is just hoping for a friend. I wind up texting him that I'm too busy to talk – that it's difficult for me to talk on phones, that I have a hearing problem, lies, whatever I can think of to stiff-arm him out of my life.

It is weeks later and I am trying to write it all up, with a beginning, a middle, and an end, trying to reanimate him from the ashes of that day. In an eerie coincidence, he texts me right as I'm typing, as I'm rendering him in a Word document – his marriage has collapsed out of nowhere. Alongside a life still being lived, the story I am writing begins to feel like a prison, its sentences walls. He tells me that he has the most dysfunctional relationship in the world with his wife, and Riley's agent has discovered Haley stealing from what he says are his offshore accounts. A notorious asshole, according to Riley, the agent at least knows how to protect his assets.

"He's Satan, but he's my Satan," Riley says over the phone, forgetting my alleged telephonic deafness, maybe just happy to have someone to talk to.

But it seems impossible, legally, in Missouri, to get married and divorced in such a short time. I research legal documents online, but can't know for sure – there is not a single shred of him anywhere on the Internet. He wants to go back to The Queen the next day. He says he's really not doing well, that he might "crack," but it feels like he's saying that just to get me back to the casino. I wonder about his mental stability – I don't know what is happening anymore. I am not his friend, but I try my best to temp as one, hoping to make him feel better. It almost feels like I owe him that after disappearing on him.

It is hard to say: from his point of view, who am I?

I can't prove he is who he says he is, but I can't disprove it either. It doesn't seem to matter anymore. After I don't hear anything else that winter, I start worrying. Is he okay? Did I wrong him somehow? Do I have an obligation to this stranger I met? I call him and there's no answer. I begin making solitary pilgrimages to the Casino Queen. On the third or fourth visit, his bartender pal tells me that Riley hasn't been there in weeks. Riley's voicemail reroutes to a recording that explains the number has disabled incoming calls. I wonder if he is dead or in a hospital somewhere. I have one last text exchange, and it starts to feel like he never existed:

> Me: "Yo I just want to know you're okay. You there?"

> Me: "Hey what's up man? You doing ok?"

> Response: "I'm sorry, I think you have the wrong number."

> Me: "Sorry if I do. Is this riley?"

> Response: "No."

•

I don't hear from him again.

My story gets workshopped and Riley is fossilized into a few autumn hours. A friend's mom begins to refer to me as Casino Queen. I tell the story of that day so often all I have left is the story. With the passage of time, my concern for him recedes back into the riddle of his identity. He is only a character now.

Almost a year later, I run into a friend in the street. He says he and some others are going to a concert that night, Would I want to come? I ask who is performing and then my jaw drops: it is Dr. John.

The concert is held in the exact spot where I first met Riley, near the Arch, which doesn't seem itself at night, starved of sun, dimmed and grayed. I am finally going to see the truth for myself, one last litmus test of reality: a sound engineer would be working the concert of his employer.

I see fragments of Riley everywhere. I see him by the stage, then behind a gate. But no tattoos. I leave behind everyone I've come with, wandering around on my own. I am a madman fascinated by the human wrist. He isn't here and I feel like a fool to think I could find him again. Then I think I see him in the more expensive seating section. As everyone gazes out at the stage, I stand by the section's perimeter, looking back at the crowd, squinting. He is a younger-looking guy amidst a generally older fan base; Dr. John is now in his 70s.

Maybe his hair is too different, too bright. Then I realize the color is just highlights. It has been so long, it's hard to remember. I'm thinking back to the story I wrote, sifting through its pages to drag out details and test them against the people of the crowd. Then this guy with highlighted hair stands up during "Right Place, Wrong Time," the song Riley had told me was his favorite – about someone for whom everything is always a bit off-kilter – and I know I've found him. In a metropolitan area of three million people, there he is. Even from far away I can see the writing on his wrists.

When he at last moves through the crowd, I fling myself after him, bowling over old ladies, I imagine now, ducking underneath clots of Dr. John fans, thrashing my way through swaths of meaningless strangers until he is right in front of me, with his goofy, mischievous smile and one more cigarette.

"Hey Riley!" I say crazily.

He looks me over.

"I love Dr. John," he says after a nanosecond of hesitation.

There is a sense of blankness, as if his jubilant hello is only a triggered response, the pulling of some deep internal lever. But he is way less twitchy than in the casino. Sobered. Riley says he quit the band to get healthy after an overdose of Everclear liquor.

"I was out of control," he tells me, sadly. "Dr. John is on heroin right now."

I see scars on Riley's arm that I hadn't noticed a year before. My story was called *The River* and maybe the real Riley had drowned in it. Maybe it is drugs after all. I make my big confession and tell him I've written about him for a workshop. He doesn't mind. I ask why he hasn't been back to the Home of the Loosest Slots.

"The bartenders are what's loose," he says.

Now he is saying he had sex with Twanya. In spite of the oddness of it all, I am feeling nostalgic, like we shared something long ago. I can see he is too. He is still talking about beating people up, but he says he was banned from The Queen for flirting too much with one of the bartenders. He goes to a different casino now.

We happen to be near yet another one – the giant emerald fin of the Lumiere Casino shadows over us. The concert volume increases and it becomes harder to hear over Dr. John's scratchy voice. Riley buys us shots, a few milliliters of alcohol in plastic containers that are usually used for soy sauce. He can't get his open, can't pry open the lid, so he just slams it into his face, the liquid dribbling down his chin. Not once does he allude to anything I haven't alluded to. There is a new band he talks about now, one with his name. Riley is the lead singer. This catches me off guard. Lead singer? I am overcome with a need to find some kind of answer, to balance the complex equation of his identity. I remember he told me when we first met that he had a young child, only two years old, a son named Aidan.

"What was the name of your daughter again?" I ask casually.

He tells me without hesitation.

"Jessica."

Maybe in the next moment he describes Jessica in detail. Maybe he lists her age, habits, a cute first word. But I don't know because I hole up in my head, processing, remembering, recalibrating. The night feels colder all of a sudden and the gusts of wind off the river give me a sensation of repeatedly waking up. When I return to the moment, I ask more questions and get new answers: he doesn't seem to be from Alabama. He references a girlfriend named Ashley, which is almost an anagram of Haley. I gently remind him of things he said the day we met and he seems stuck. His sentences are all false starts and I stop prodding.

"Honestly, my parents are here," he says at one point.

"Obviously they've met Dr. John," he says at another.

No mention of divorce, much less a marriage. No child. Riley is at the concert with his parents, who have taken him to see his favorite guitarist: he's a big fan.

He is more reticent now, this man who told me tall tales of totaling six cars, of knocking out six teeth – this man behind the curtain is a boy with a Simpson's-themed email address. I think back to my conception of him that day, as this larger-than-life figure, some kind of Tasmanian devil of the St. Louis underground, and it is difficult to square the two. We are who people allow us to be.

I don't press him on any of it – I think of how happy he was that day, the day he could be whoever he wanted. What a way to meet someone – there is a lot of reality in the sinews of fantasy. I am unprepared for how pervasive the lying is, though, how practically none of it is true, and what may be underneath that.

We decide we'll head to a bar, but as we're walking to the train, the same one from a year before, I decide I can't go with him, that I shouldn't separate him from his parents – I feel protective over this new Riley. He seems hurt that the night will end early, that we will not climb back into the jagged rabbit hole of his favorite life story. Even now, years later, it strikes me that he was willing to leave the concert of a man he worshipped. I take him back to the music. He runs the last few yards bent over, arms extended as wings, like even the little while he was gone was too long.

In that moment, we shrink back to smaller versions of ourselves. I've been living a fantasy too, fulfilling a particular idea of myself, an embedded writer, a detective, an adventurer in knowing people and not knowing them. That summer, I am a copywriting intern working out of a supply closet. I compose flavorless institutional propaganda related to sustainability. Riley and I look at each other one last time. Across the parking lot, we wave.

VI

NO MORE POSTCARDS

"I hope the memory of your last New Year's Eve is one that stays with you for the long haul. I think that I love remembering people, or particular moments with people, more than I enjoy having been with them in the first place, and I wonder if you and I are alike in this capacity. Or maybe it's just that I like the ability to control something, like keeping those moments locked up in a bottle. The clearest example of this in my own life is the fact that I told you the people at grad school were the ones I was waiting all my life for. I'm not friends with many of them now. But I still love them for having been."

BY CHANCE

When we are little, my friend's dad drives us north, to his college reunion. The last hour or so of the ride, he would play a game, the same one every year. Whenever there is a fork in the road, he won't turn until we pick a direction. Somehow, whichever ways we choose, we always guess right. We always get there. There must be some secret, an underlying geographical sorcery of the road, but I didn't know it then, and I don't know it now.

Eventually we stop going, stop guessing, we all get older. But it made its imprint as a kind of magic, as elemental as the heat of the bonfire once we finally arrive, its charring, burning wood alongside the coldest air I'd ever known up till then.

I think of those drives the other day, when I see a very old woman at a playground turning a steering wheel attached to a jungle gym. First she hangs her shopping bag on a rail, and then turn, turn, turn. Her adult son is there with his dog, off the leash, giving her space, but always watching.

We lose touch, this friend and I – that's how things go – but I thought we'd find our way back to each other. That we'd chat about little things you preserve when you're veterans of the same past. But then one day I get a phone call and I have to figure out how to get to the funeral. I try to talk to him in dreams sometimes, but since I don't really know him anymore, he doesn't say anything to me. Not a word – that's how long it's been. The best

I can do is put a single gray soldier from our battered RISK set on my shelf, in private memorial.

I guess sometimes you don't get there. Too many turns.

THE MESSENGER

L. and I are not speaking due to a mutual self-imposed silence I refer to as Indefinite Exile. We laugh about this, a last laugh of sorts, since we know it is just a fancy phrase describing forever. When we leave the waffle place, there is one more kiss, and we each keep looking over our shoulders as we walk away. Now her old housemate is in New York staying in my apartment. We talk about many things but never her. Still, sometimes it feels like I am speaking to her by proxy. I am smuggling information to her in these séances, hoping she can hear. I know she will ask him what I said, so it is almost like she is there, like it will reach her. The idea of her knowing the scenes and stories of my life fills me with happiness, so I go on and on. I tell him about the park I go to that was an official gift from Greece to the neighborhood, the risky career move I made, that at the very end of Steinway Street, the piano factory is still there.

We talk about desire, the way it happens across a space. A little after her birthday I get drunk and text him, not her. I want to know if she had a nice time.

When we are eating in a restaurant, he takes out his phone to use a decibel meter app that measures noise. He is a violinist, so he has always been interested in sound. Lately, he's been measuring noise wherever he goes.

"There is always noise," he says, even if you can't quite hear it. Always a lesser noise layered under the one you're hearing. "Without noise," he says, "you go crazy."

I don't know it yet, but they are not as close as they

once were. They are not even speaking any more. When I find out, I mourn all these details never trafficked to her, and sit there in shock. I'm reminded of something she once said when we were together.

"There is no such thing as catching up."

Summaries are just Band-Aids smothering an absence. The fact remains: you've missed it.

I still text him, but I don't ask about her anymore. Something else happens – he sends me marmalade from his garden. I edit his grad school thesis. He makes an InDesign fix on my first business card. Then one day we are driving through his home country Taiwan, up one of its greenest and steepest mountain ranges. We ring the narrow road higher and higher – the long way is the only way here. We drive through miles of cloud, and I wake up in a realm of white. I feel lucky to be in this holy place. When we at last reach the peak, a Goldenwing soars upward and perches on my shoulder for just a second. That sense of grip, the flush of good fortune, an unexpected friend.

THE LOFT

"I used to think you were cool," my little brother says.

Now that he is away at college and I don't live at home, our schedules don't overlap as much anymore. Maybe the distance lets him view me differently. We are five years apart, and he used to always look up to me.

One of our childhood traditions was playing *NHL '04* on GameCube. We bet five dollars a game, and in marathon sessions, fortunes are won and lost. We play in a room in our apartment everyone refers to as "the loft" even though it's not elevated. They call it that because I always called it that, because when I was younger that's what I thought a loft was, a cozy place in which you have fun.

My mom sometimes gets upset when she hears yelling, if my brother and I are fighting, but we deal with it ourselves. We can seal the sliding door to this little loft, soundproofed in our own sonic universe.

Sometimes he wins and sometimes I win, but my favorite part of playing is celebrating after I score. I shout out some joking corruption of the player's name, some reference to who knows what; I am the goofiest version of myself around my brother. I don't know that I'm even capable of sharing that side of me with anyone else. It's a flavor of euphoria, an acceptable ridiculousness, a throwing away of my more conscious masks. Now that he's older though, my goofiness embarrasses him, even when there's no one around.

I score with lots of players but most often with Left Winger Shane Doan, a "gritty" forward, according to the game's announcer.

"Welcome to Doanland!" I say the first time Doan puts the puck in the net.

"One visit wasn't enough?" I tease my brother when I score again.

"Population three," I shout after the third goal. "Real estate market is pickin' up heat."

He used to think my naming jokes were funny, but now he thinks they're dumb. So dumb, he threatens to tape record my outbursts and send them to someone if I don't stop. Sometimes when he scores, he nicknames his players too. Sometimes he still laughs, but mostly he acts embarrassed.

Over the years, we play less and less. The game is formulaic; it gets old. Our dog Indy nibbles on one of the joysticks; buttons no longer work.

One day I am trying to buy something on eBay, but my password isn't working. I barely use it anymore – it's my account now only in name, because my brother uses it way more often. But I find something I want, so I ask him for the new password. He texts it to me: Doanland.

PHANTOM FRIENDSHIPS

She is asking me if we can go get some chocolate. Again.
This friend always wants chocolate, anything chocolate.
Bars, cakes, ice creams. In Duane Reades, in the restaurants of luxury hotels. Once we went from the East Village to the Upper East Side just for some hot lava cake –
it's fair to say that our friendship revolves almost entirely around long walks and conversations with chocolate-related detours. We rarely include other people. She herself says it is a friendship of intense connections and then lengthy periods of disconnection: in a way the friendship is only alive when we're together, in the time before we each recede into unimportance. Sometimes I think we have cravings for each other too. Or maybe it is just that we live in different boroughs, caught between geographical distance and emotional closeness.
The walks are mainly transfers of information about our lives, commentaries about things. At some point I notice that she delays revealing her best news, like holding onto an ace in poker. Slow-playing her life. I'm with her for two hours, and then she tells me she got a new job.

"You conduct our interactions like a play," I say.
"There is always another scene to be revealed."

"Otherwise it would get boring," she says.

We have so many of these walks and so many of these talks that we feel very close to each other. We pledge that when the summer comes, we'll live together. I am serious about my roommates; it's a sacred thing to me, like we're intertwining the strings of our destinies.

The summer arrives, she returns from a trip, and we are walking from Union Square to where I live, the whole three miles. We are going to my house so I can give her back a key I borrowed. In a walk this long, the transitions between neighborhoods are more salient. By the time we reach Times Square, we are moving through thickets of skin. Sad news slithers around the conveyor belt on 42nd and neon pours down from above. As we're walking, I ask about housing. Our plan.

She has some news, she says. I hear the word "Unfortunately." Afterward, she'll say she'd like a candy bar, and she'll ask if I'd like one too. No thanks, I'll reply, but she'll keep asking.

"Are you sure I can't get you one?"

She has agreed to live with other people in the time we were apart. Two guys. They have asked her and she has said yes.

HOW YOU'LL KNOW

Go to another country and find the only other person in your house who isn't a devout Christian. Wander the streets until the two of you find a cafe. Take the chessboard but don't worry that there are no pieces. Use what you have instead. What you have is coins. When you win, she'll fashion you a homemade trophy out of copper-toned wrapper. Keep it.

Start taking walks to an abandoned train yard and let her show you how her old camera works. Tell her about the movies you like and don't make her feel bad for not knowing some of them even though she's the one who studies film. Sit on the platform while the train thunders beneath.

Call it "getting fucked by a train."

When she tells you your bikelessness is a problem because she wants to go places, get a bike. Get it even though the brake is broken and it appears to be stolen, smuggled in by a gang of notorious local thieves.

When you are at a party, she will tell you she loves you, but that she tends to disappear. Let her go.

When something stressful comes up and she is keeping you waiting, walk back up the stairs and find her beside her bed counting pennies. Don't get annoyed that she's making you really late. Sit down on the floor and help her count them. Stack the pennies and watch the copper move higher and higher. By the time the stacks are tall towers, she will be calm and you can go.

Listen to what she says while you're riding your bikes side by side. Listen closely. She will tell you a story she was telling someone else in which you are a character. She will mention you as a "close friend," and that's how you'll know.

Don't forget that is how friendship moves, by intermittent tiny lurches, assumption by assumption until they come true.

Go to Germany with your friend and walk along what's left of the wall. Dodge the homeless man who spits at you for no reason. Hitch a ride to Munich with an erratic driver and thank god you have your friend in the back seat. Spend a whole week with her before she gets embarrassed that she's told so many stories, she says she has none left.

"Jason, I think I'm all out," she'll say, like your friend is a car that's on empty.

Say her name too, and make sure to laugh. Tell her that's when things get interesting.

THE GREEN THAT'S LEFT

We are the only people on the platform. If there were any others, my memory has shoved them onto the tracks into insignificance. A massive man approaches, eyeing my plastic bag full of four-leaf clovers. From the valley of the train station, downtown St. Louis looks big and corporate and gray. My clovers are fresh and green.

He asks me what I'm holding, so I tell him.

"Nah, those are extinct," he says.

I found them all the way at the end of the train line in Shiloh, Illinois. There's an air force base and a lot of nothing. In the nothing are fields, which is where I found them.

What he says next catches me off guard too: he wants to know if I'm Irish. I'm confused until I see him studying me and my red beard, possibly concluding that I'm an urban leprechaun. The man admires the beauty of the clovers and suggests that I laminate them. We continue to talk as we wait – he wants to know if I like to party. I consider my answer for what feels like a long time, but he pulls a sometimes out of me: sometimes I drink, I say. Sometimes I smoke.

Turns out he can get me some good cocaine.

The man seems not to hear my No Thanks. He tells me he deals to support his four-year-old daughter. I will never forget her name. All five syllables. I think I tell him it's a beautiful name – if I didn't, at least that thought passed through my mind.

Forget the heavy frontage of Midwestern How Are Yous – in my St. Louis, it feels like the wall between strangers is very thin, thinning the longer I am there, the deeper in I go. It started with Riley, and it hasn't stopped. The sheer amount of times the conversation somehow goes straight to the gut. It strikes me most years later when I'm talking with a girl from Hong Kong. In hyper-dense, high-rise-laden Hong Kong, she will say, strangers exist so you can make transactions with them.

"Why would you talk to them? Hong Kongers don't ask questions. It's nosy. It's rude. You wouldn't strike up a conversation. When I came here," she said, meaning the United States, "I didn't know how to respond to people."

I ask the man what he does for a living, because maybe the drug dealing is only a small part of what he does. He thinks I'm insulting him, and he gives me a scary look, like I crossed a line.

"I already told you," he says. "I want to be judged for who I am; not what I do."

Right then he asks for my number so he can get me the cocaine, so we can transact. To seal the deal.

"Sorry," I say. "I'm leaving St. Louis soon." Very soon.

And I will – I'll move back home, neutering a spirit of exploration, of openness. I'll be saturated in what I already know, in the places I've already been, and I'll curse myself for it.

"I thought we were going to break bread together," he says.

The meal we will never share hangs there between us until he breaks the silence.

"I know you're gonna give me one of them clovers. Let me get some of that luck."

Before she moved away, L. went with me to the end of the line, out of Missouri into Illinois. No one we knew had ever been to the end of the line. A trip to nowhere, we went just to go. There was nothing there, which was the best thing that could've been there. She found her four-leaf clovers so easily, one then two then three. For me it was harder. On my hands and knees, scrutinizing the green clover by clover. When I found one – when I saw the fourth leaf – I was so happy I screamed. When she left, I went back, all the way to Illinois. I didn't know where else to go. When we spoke about the possibility of us ever reuniting, we agreed we were leaving it up to chance – to steer us back together or not. Maybe we would get lucky, but in fiction, chance is often viewed as a cop-out. Maybe in life it is too.

It is hard to think with the man standing so close to me, and I waver, but I say no. Later I realize he is pressing me because maybe he needs them. Maybe he believes they hold real power.

I am thinking I will give them to people I know. People I love. Eventually, I will give one to L. But when I give it to her, it won't mean what I hoped it would. She already has so many. I know not to dwell on these memories of before the end – I know to let them fade, these memories that shimmer with joy and clouds and fields and the winding road. Only two skinny red signs by Shiloh warn cars they are going the wrong way.

I put the other clovers between two thin pieces of display glass, as though they are ornamental. But now, when I look, it is hard to believe so little of the green is left. How much of it is gone, how much has yellowed. I imagine a syringe needle has been stuck into each delicate leaf, the pigment somehow extracted over the years and now nearing a full fade, at last. It's difficult to extricate them from the memory of L. What was once the closest connection I'd ever had disintegrated into the occasional text between strangers.

I tell the man I'm sorry, but no.

"It's just a clover," I think, but how can I say that? It's not just a clover to me either. It's believing in things. An earnestness. We are fellow passengers of that sincerity, I see now. Comrades, even. I hope luck found him anyway.

We stand there waiting for the train and the conversation moves on. It turns out he used to live in New York and has come back to St. Louis to be closer to family. I live in St. Louis, but I am going back to New York to be closer to family. I am taking the eastern line. He is taking the western one. We look at each other, agreeing that we seem to be on a similar parallel of life's mystic map. We shake hands. When the train arrives, we go our separate ways.

SOME THINGS YOU CAN'T HOLD

I've met someone new. We want to go hiking, but neither of us has a car, so we settle for walking the George Washington Bridge, no one's favorite. It is a fixture though, speared deep into rock on both sides of the water. It seems so solid, the bridge, so much of itself, one color, the sky on a forgettable day – solid. The George Washington is the most trafficked bridge in the world. This high, I'm trying to trick my brain, trying to distract it – the river is something I won't survive. I tell myself not to compare with L. Not to think of past intimacies. I know to look outward, lost in the view, or inward, at the barrier between the cars and me. Here are the very bones of the bridge, fortified with metal. There are scattered shards all around, bolts and screws, strewn across the cement. I take one, because some things you can't hold in your hands. We are having such a good time. The bolt is surprisingly heavy, flavored with orange rust, the circular slither of its screws ringing it like the age of a tree. Is this the work of the bridge, I wonder, expunging parts of itself it doesn't need, littering out its life?

Or is it full of holes?

THE BEEP

I am his tutor and he is trying to tell me about an unknown variable. About X. But he has forgotten that it's called X.

"The mysterious thing," he says, laughing.

I love him for this. I will tell everyone I know about the mysterious thing.

During one session we're in his apartment and I hear a beep. Just one beep. The microwave, probably.

"I'm really sorry," he tells me, tensing up.

Sorry for what? It feels like I'm missing something.

"Totally fine!"

On the walk home I wonder why he was so on edge. Then I forget about it, my thoughts about him confined to the tiny sliver of the week we share. In the middle of another session, his mom comes home. She sits next to him, asks how it's going. He's taken the wrong test, so we're a little behind.

"I wish I had a baseball bat," she says, smiling.

I see her smiling, so I automatically smile too, before I process what she might mean. Then she makes another comment, this time about throwing him off the roof. She smiles again.

I don't know what I can say. Or do. Or if I'm just crazy. So far on the outside of something I can't really see it. I say it's not a big deal, the test. Not at all. He is doing well. Very well.

Sometimes I think about the beep. I also think he is okay, but I don't really know. I'm not his tutor anymore.

QUOTE OF THE DAY

My cousin is detoxing next to me in the loft. There's been another relapse recently, and he isn't welcome at home anymore. I stay up late with him watching episode after episode of *Law & Order*, medicinal in its formula and tidy closures. A break, at any rate, from being offered heroin in the parking lot outside your NA group.

What I learn that night is that sometimes there is intimacy to be won in not talking about something. Disclosures emerge from the void – stuff I'd never known. He's legally blind in one eye, and actually wore a patch as a kid to strengthen it. One of his dreams was to become a photographer for *National Geographic*. He wishes he'd gotten a chance to go to college, even if it were a scholarship to "some shit school."

Later, his dad tells me he stops getting emails from him, and all contact falls off. It's hard to watch the distance grow in real time, seeing one and then the other, but not together. Both sides tell stories of betrayal.

I am one of the people who occasionally fills in for support. I stop by at an arraignment, and it's unnerving to hear the hushed echo of public defenders calling out their clients' names right before the cases are called. The slapdash nature of the whole thing. The speedy wheel of fate.

"Ben —?"

"John —?"

"Cameron —?"

Right after a lawyer finally locates and meets my cousin, he trades him to a different lawyer because of a scheduling conflict. Luckily, the second lawyer is savvy, and the charges are reduced.

For a while, his dad, my uncle, has been sending out a Quote of the Day to an email group of family and friends. A way to share some of the wisdom he's accrued. When it arrives, it always feels like a small but meaningful gift. After the quotes stop for a few days, though, it isn't the kind of thing I even notice.

Someone does though. And shoots over an email for the first time in a long time. My cousin. His son.

"Where are my quotes?"

THE BOX

It's Christmas, and my mom is making French toast to busy her mind. We usually go to a movie so the time passes quickly. It's 23 years since my mom's mom died, and the day it happened is the day every year that she slips back into the worst of her grief.

During breakfast, I ask to hear more about my grandmother. I know very little, I've realized, even though she was my mom's best friend, and she meant everything to her. I know that she taught braille even though she was partially blind herself. One of her students loved her so much that when it was time for the school to switch itinerant teachers, his family fought the school, and the family won. Many years later, all grown up, the student drove across the state from college to her funeral.

When my mom was pregnant, a friend recommended that she get a particular kind of slippers. For some reason, these slippers were important to her; it became important that she have them. But on the day that I was born, someone had forgotten them. It was her mom who remembered, and she brought them just in time.

I like this story, and am glad to hear it a second time, even a third, but in these stories my grandmother is always mute. I have never heard her voice. There are pictures of us when I was two, the year she died. We are on someone's deck; it must be hers. I look happy and so does she. It is a strange feeling to miss someone you've never known. There are videos of her, but they are silent films, scored with music.

"What did she sound like?" I ask.

Just one phrase, so I can get some sense of her. I also want to know why my mom can't remember a single thing she used to say, but I have chosen the wrong day to get to know my grandmother and quibble about stories without dialogue.

My mom takes it as an attack, and maybe it is. Her stress has been building – this is not what she needs.

"I have a lot on my mind," she says. "I have so much on my mind."

I can hear her in the other room on the phone, screaming at my dad, hoarse with panic.

"Where is my box?"

"Where did you put it?"

She can't find the box that contains all the things she wrote down about her mom that she remembered.

"You'll forget," someone told her.

ALL THESE LITTLE THINGS

I am in England when my great-grandmother dies. I will miss the funeral and my mom will read me the eulogy over the phone. My grandmother's mom – 99 years old. My mom is in New York the day it happens. She's coming home from one of her dad's tag sales, where she helps out. When she's back, she has to pick something up before six from a repair store on our block. The store is tiny: essentially a large closet with a hoarder's assemblage of every type of tool. The men there fix shoes, pocket books, broken straps, all these little things. For 20 years my mom has gone to this same repair shop and chatted with these same guys. She is distraught and finds herself telling one of the repairmen what happened.

"I feel like I lost the last part of my mom today," she tells him.

"No," the repairman says. "You're the last part of your mom."

VII

THE MAN ON THE STREET

A man with garbage bags slung over his shoulder asks me if I have any change. I'm on my lunch break at a new job I don't like, walking back to 23rd Street in the gross heat of this New York City July. Out on the sidewalk, even though the man with the bags seems to be in actual despair, I can say I'm sorry and keep walking, which is what I do. But then I stop and walk back. Maybe a fluky rupture in the firewall I've grown over a lifetime of these types of exchanges. A sense that my autopilot is taking me somewhere I don't want to go. Or maybe there have been too many trips on the sadness trains where person after person clears their throat and apologizes for taking up your time and tells you about the job they lost and a house without heat and no house at all and how they had a family once and how they wish more than anything they didn't have to ask but they need something to eat tonight. This man's hands are plunged into a trash bin seeking recyclables, but what he really needs is his medicine, he says. I tell him I'll buy him lunch, let's go. I say that sometimes I write, that one thing I try to write about is people who are overlooked. This makes sense to him, but he doesn't want lunch. If he eats, his whole body will shut down. He needs water. Water is his food.

"I'm burnin' out," he says over and over again.

For the next few hours, we go through the routines

of his day: the bottle dispensaries, the dumpsters, the resting spots, he takes me through it all, talks me through where he's been. Never knew his father. He was born in New York, where his mom raised him before taking him to St. Thomas. He returned in his early 20s, my age when I meet him. He is 53, the same age as my dad.

His New York is not the star-studded center of the universe it is sometimes perceived to be.

"It's not all that. Not the place you really think," he says.

He has a roller duffel bag he calls his house. "F. Joshua" is scribbled in black across the bag's faded red. His things are less possessions than things he carries: bundles of *National Geographic*s someone threw out, some clothes, his blanket, an umbrella, some pennies he'll roll up and trade in at the bank. With a bad back, there is only so much he can handle. He doesn't begrudge anyone who can't help him out with a dollar or two.

"Everybody got a different opinion. I don't really got an opinion – I just see it for what it is: You gotta survive, you gotta live, you gotta eat."

He prefers to do it in the street. They make that announcement on the subway, "Please don't give." And anyway there's too many people down there.

"I don't know who is who," he says.

I decide not to go back to work today. I watch his stuff while he goes to the bathroom in a Starbucks. Then I watch his stuff so he can change his clothes and take a quick shower. Often he'll pass out and wake up with his possessions gone. He has no one to guard them; his bag used to be a cart. He limps to different safe spots, camouflaging certain possessions in garbage so he can return to them later – small strategic gambles. He used to have a companion – "my man Ray." They would cook on the highway, but he hasn't seen him for a while.

"I don't really have nobody," he says.

When he was younger he cleaned floors and un-loaded trucks. He was a janitor when he started using cocaine. He robbed a taxi driver, was bused upstate to prison until he got out and there was no money left.

"Did you do it?" I ask about the robbery.

"Yes, I did it," he says.

He has been homeless for decades now, through Koch, Dinkins, Giuliani, and Bloomberg. He says he's constantly hassled by police, searched often and falsely accused. Since his mom died, there hasn't been anyone to support him. There's a close relative but she doesn't really help – the one who got him hooked on cocaine, he says. We are standing beside a mountain range of U-Haul trash bags in the back lot of Manhattan Mini Storage, looking for what he calls the "poor man's treasure."

When mini-storage renters don't pay their monthly bills, U-Haul disposes of their possessions, but before the truck takes them all away, Franklin Joshua arrives. He sifts through bags, patting them on the sides like he is frisking someone. The items are random, forgotten for who knows what reason. There are Christmas ornaments for a holiday that wasn't celebrated, shrink-wrapped and never hung. The grand prize is the jewelry. The key is to keep your eye out for anything that glints. The brilliant specks.

We look together, finding single shoes and looking for their siblings. He pours rubbing alcohol into centimeter-deep crevices in his palms, then shakes them to stop the burning. It's the best way he knows how to get clean – it's how he survives, as this knowing scaven-ger. Even his cigarettes he gets from half-smoked ones abandoned on the ground. I think of Riley moving his heel over the discards.

I give him some money for his medicine. He's been without it for two days and his whole body – part by part – is becoming numb. I am happy to give it to him: I know he will stretch it so much further than I ever could. Technically I am being paid for being with him. I am on the clock, so this money, he can have it.

We are both prodigious walkers, but I never know where I am going and he seems to have a photographic spatial memory, like a London cabbie whose hippocampus has grown far beyond its normal size from driving around so much. As we walk, more and more things come up. The city is his house, his life, and we are walking through it. His streets are filled with This used to be Thats. His streets are filled with people who yell at him.

"Get the fuck outta here."

"Get a job."

He completes odd jobs for which he is rarely paid, receiving the lowly dishonor of being stiffed after scrubbing up rat shit. A 24-hour car wash in Chelsea won't hire American. Once, just once, he lucked into a job as an artist's overseer. Twenty-one dollars an hour, he remembers.

"An hour."

But one day, the artist went berserk. High on crystal meth, he'd locked himself out of his gallery and asked Joshua for a hammer from his cart. The artist smashed through his own glass window and the police had to come. They are still friends, but he moved away. Sometimes he sends money from Canada; he helps how he can. It was the best job Joshua ever had. There was a movie made about the artist, he says, and he, Franklin Joshua, was in it.

I am skeptical. A movie?

He is unfailingly polite to anyone he comes across, in a way that seems instinctual rather than calculated for pity. If he bumps into someone with his aggregated wingspan of garbage bags: "So sorry."

Around areas he forages, he offers to help any way he can.

"No charge, boss."

Eventually we are in a park, sitting at a table, one of the ones with the green and white chess squares painted into the concrete. We say our goodbyes as he rolls up his pennies. When I am in Chelsea now I keep my eye out, but I haven't seen him. Later, it will be winter and one night I meet up with a friend at a Hot & Crusty near my house. We're just sitting there, deep in the evening, and I find myself thinking of Joshua. The story is up, it's been published, but he's still out there.

•

I can't quite forget him. People flicker back to us; they fade in and out. When Franklin Joshua and I are walking around his New York and I am asking him about some things, he is telling me about his days. He says he likes fishing, which catches me off guard. I ask him what he likes about it to rustle up some detail, to fill him out, to make his character not so thin.

He looks at me like I'm dumb, a child, like that's such a stupid question.

"I just like it," he says, as I laugh at myself.

•

At home, I find the movie he mentioned – a documentary – on YouTube. I remember what he's told me about his friendship with the artist, which started as a random interaction in the street. Eventually, the artist trusts Joshua enough to get some money out of the ATM for him.

"My mind was not to come back with the credit card," Joshua tells me. "I got a pin number and I got a credit card. He sent me to withdraw 600 dollars which came out *like that*."

But while he was waiting for the bus to make his getaway, he changed his mind. "My mind hit me," he remembers, "and I'm like 'wait a minute, where you goin' with the man's credit card and his money?'" He was on 13th Street between Washington Street and 9th Avenue. It was 12 years ago.

Out of his decision grew an unlikely friendship.

Drawing Out the Demons records the artist's last days in New York. The film covers his lowest, rawest nadir, but lingers long enough to observe his parents using the last of their money to invest in his recovery. It concludes with a humbled, thoughtful version of the artist, working again in Canada. Joshua does in fact appear, two minutes worth of a cameo, stretched over a few weeks' time. He is younger, fuller, healthier, infused with more energy. He even rides a bike the artist gives him, able to secure it with a heavy iron chain. But for Joshua, there is no narrative of change. What stands out is the sameness. The euphoria of the bike acquisition is blotted out by the abrupt loss of every single one of his possessions. As a distressed Joshua recounts to his friend the hauling of his property into the trash, the drugged artist responds tonelessly.

"Life is shitty, isn't it?"

•

When I listen to the recording of our interaction, the streets are noisy, the garbage trucks grunt, the cars clear their throats, but the basement of the Western Beef is even louder – the destruction of each bottle, the shifting plastic seas inside the machine.

In the bowels of the market, Joshua packs bottles and cans into a recycling machine, turning them into smaller, flattened versions of themselves. He shares a few Way Back Whens with some Western Beef employees, all of them smiling, nodding, remembering, surrounded by stacks of factory-sealed Fiji Water and Orange Crush. He used to sleep on the highway, where they'd throw away some of the meat and he'd cook it there in wintertime with Ray, as the snow fell.

Joshua is telling me then about his mom. The only one who always stuck by him. Because the recently deceased Eunice Maria Joshua raised her kids alone, she decided they should take her last name. He wears it like a badge, a surname turned into a first name. As Joshua deposits his bottles beneath Western Beef, some accepted by the machine, some with their bar codes illegible, discarded on the floor, he tells me his mom made a family member promise she would look after him when she was gone. "She has not kept that promise," he says. When he tells me his mom is dead, how he explains it, it sounds like she's still around, just far away.

"She's not here no more," he says.

He can't understand how the machines won't accept the very same bottles that the store sells. Why they won't take them. It is here in the basement that he tells me what keeps him going, which day will be different finally from the other days. He tells me he's trying to win the local lottery. He plays the number from the year his mother was born, 1936, has played it every day since she died. He only won once, just a dollar. But one day – one day, he says, "I'm going to hit it straight and the day I hit it straight I got $2,500. I'm gonna buy me a ticket and buy flowers, 12 flowers, and go to St. Thomas and put them on top of her grave."

VIII

THAT THING YOU SAID

"This is my last night at the hostel. I think I mentioned that my flight's in a few hours."

"I lived in many hostels in my life. I lived in Sicily three months in a hostel. I lived in Japan in a hostel cause it's cheap, it's a good way to meet people, you can cook. I've been kicked out of so many places in my life. I'm used to it. My brother has been telling me for the last 30 years that I am childish. It may be the truth. When I was 13, my parents kicked me out, so I think maybe I got stuck there. Because the way I blew all that money was childish. Without thinking."

"The Jaguar and —

"Yeah, everything. I'm down to $2,000 if I sell my car, and I have two expensive flutes…"

"…And okay what's very particular about music is that you cannot see it and you cannot touch it. It's here. So, when I perform, I don't say a word. I play and I go from one instrument to the other. Somebody introduces me, and at the end I talk to the people. I tell stories about the lives of all the composers. Because I read biographies. Mozart. Beethoven. Bach. Goethe. Wolfgang means the walk of the wolf. And

the two Wolfgangs met! Goethe went to listen to Mozart. And he congratulated Mozart."

"The walk of the wolf."

"Yeah, the walk of the wolf."

"I love that. That sounds like you a little bit."

"Oh, yeah, completely."

"Never totally finding a home. Always moving. On the outsides."

"Well, because I'm a Buddhist my home is on the inside. And this is why I don't mind living in a very small place."

A MATTER OF METERS, MILES, ROADS

I speak to a Chinese man on the phone sometimes. He's trying to improve his English and I need the extra cash, so we talk. About China, his life, mine, the better paying job he is hoping for. We talk exclusively in paid shifts of conversation, usually 30 minutes or an hour.

If he makes an error, I am supposed to correct it. Usually, I do. Instead of "honestly," he says "truth-speaking." As in "Truth-speaking, I am not so happy." He says it sometimes but I don't correct him – I like it too much. When someone uses the word "honestly," it feels like they are quickly switching to a more candid channel, but "truth-speaking" feels like it comes from down deeper, extracted from a personal mine of candor. By not correcting him, I am the steward of this phrase, of its delicate course in the world. Another time, when he is trying to ask about my availability to talk on the phone, he asks if I'm close.

"Can you talk? Are you nearby?"

I enjoy these slight errors in translation, as though he is saying that availability is a kind of proximity. Emotion, love, generosity just a matter of meters, miles, roads.

We talk for so many months that after a while, he'd like to meet. He invites me to dinner: traditional Chinese food, his wife will cook. The problem is that he lives far away. Even though I'd like to go, I tell him I'm sorry I won't be able to make it, since I have no way of getting there.

It's no problem; he'll pick me up. He drives 30 minutes to my house, 30 minutes to his. He takes me into the basement, giddy to show me the rifle he seems to use exclusively for scaring the squirrels that terrorize his small estate. We have a pleasant time, we thank each other for various things, but these thank yous feel so expected and so conventional that the meaning feels weaker than we intend. Then he drives me 30 minutes to my house and I feel it in the curves of the road, the tally of yellow dashes, the darkening night. He drives 30 minutes back.

THE DAGGER

"I'll give you one guess," I tell my grandmother and my dad in Florida, after breakfast, about my favorite thing my grandfather used to say. I like to talk about him when I'm in his house.

No one has any idea, and my game is even deeper of a failure than I could've imagined. Like I've been gammoned in backgammon, like I've not only lost, but lost double. We are a family of gamers.

"I don't think he ever said that," my dad says.

"No, no," my grandmother adds.

"It's like a dagger in my heart," I remember my grandfather saying every time I'd get close to beating him in cards and lay down a particularly timely king or queen or three. Cards was the number one thing we did together. Sometimes I'd be in his room for the number two thing, which was watching basketball games. He lived in Florida and I lived in New York, so we crossed swords through the great Knicks and Heat rivalries of the 90s, boy versus man. If Patrick Ewing hit his hook shot at the end, my grandfather would clutch his heart, every time with an actor's sense of drama.

"Like a dagger," he'd croak.

I know so little about my own grandfather. I know that he had two bypasses, and part of his leg vein was coiled around his withered heart. He took what seemed like 50 pills every morning. Did I make the dagger up? His greatest weakness, his heart, reforged as an artifact of friendship in my memory?

I never got to ask him anything about his life and he never got to see me grow up. The dagger is the thing that most animates my grandfather in my memory now that he's been gone for years. He loved little competitions, little contests. I did too. He wanted to bet with my grandmother on everything they did together. Golf, ping pong, cards, each game worth a dollar. My grandmother liked winning, but he seemed so happy when he won, she liked that too.

"I won again!" he would tell their caretaker, before making another tally on one of his little golf cards.

All that's left of him in his house now are photographs. Widowhood is just a little bit easier with fewer of his things around. There used to be two closets, one for him and one for her, but now he has been reduced to a drawer. I tend to miss him almost exclusively when I visit, and then I miss him a lot, and I try to look for him. I search the whole house, but all I can find are his golf pencils.

He was a reserved man even though he ran a large paper company. He only had one rule: we were forbidden from touching his silver hair. I was a shy, quiet kid who was sometimes scared of adults, but he was so kid-like himself, he was easy for me to be around, a grown-up I was really comfortable with.

"Uhh," he'd go in mock pain, clutching his heart, as if this time I'd really got him.

I find one of his golf clubs, but it turns out it isn't the one he loved, the club of clubs that he held throughout all his years. No one can find it. My brain supplies me with the fact that in the *Oxford English Dictionary*, a word is assigned a dagger icon once it has become officially obsolete. My dad and I almost miss our flight in a desperate scramble to ship the less meaningful golf club from suburban Florida. Back in New York, I race to my mom, the confidant of my younger years.

"Of course I remember the dagger," she says.

My mom's memory is notoriously unreliable and singularly supportive of me, though. I don't trust it. As if her brain has Monet on retainer to make everything beautiful. I ask my dad for a copy of the notes I wrote for him after my grandfather died, of every single thing I could remember about his dad, all the idle, random moments I could pull up from my mental pockets. I was the one who told my brother what happened, and we both started laughing even though we didn't find it funny. The first death of anyone in our lives. I'd just graduated from high school and I went to Central Park to write it, wishing there was more I could remember, or more I'd known. I brought a notebook, but I was only able to fill two pages.

"Papa died today," I wrote, the ink smudged with rain.

The dagger was at the top of the next page. It was a relief, like I could keep the little I had left, but it was also obvious how much of what I'd known I'd loaded into that symbol, the knife also representing everything I've forgotten – when he limped through the rain to see me during my bar mitzvah. Marveling at my Lego cities. Teaching me how to hold his golf club, the only grip I've ever known. Even if it's mini golf, the grip I still use.

THE THREE HUSBANDS

We are substitutes. Their families are far away, or long gone, and there is also the matter of their arthritic hands. They can no longer write down their own stories to share, so they need scribes. I wheel an elderly woman down to the cafeteria, where the writing workshop is held. Just then, teenagers arrive by bus for their community service hours, and though they are each supposed to partner with a resident, no one chooses my charge, who is sitting alone at one of the tables. I avoid her too, since she's scowling and has her arms crossed while the rest of the room is a festival of hugs. I'd hoped to be matched with someone eager to plunge into the past to see what they find, but with the joyful storytellers claimed so quickly, I surrender and sit across from the woman I wheeled down. Within seconds, she is eyeing the exit. There is a song playing as an introduction and the group leader is leading a series of extraordinarily active stretches. My partner points out that the rigorous exercise seems more suited to the young people, and I chuckle – she's right. I take out a paper and a pen – we are supposed to start.

"My private life is for me," she says, more than once.

I'm confused because she has come to this class many times before, and at the end, the scribes read the stories out loud for everyone to hear. Another volunteer tells me that my partner loves talking about her private life, whatever that means. I try to explain to her that this prompt isn't even about that – it relates to ancestors, any stories from the old country. But she starts talking about her three husbands, who are all dead. The life insurance.

"I took the money," she says, and we laugh.

Then I understand. Her parents died when she was young. Her only family left in the old country, she doesn't know them and they don't know her. At this point, I have moved the pad aside. How did your first husband die?

"Two cars," she says.

The lack of a verb feels even more violent. The second husband she isn't sure about, can't quite remember. Maybe he died in a car crash too, she thinks. After a while, it becomes obvious she wants to leave the workshop and does not want to stay for the readings.

"Just tell them I need my medicine," she says, looking sly.

I roll her along the interminable route back to her room, down surprisingly steep ramps, into another wing, up an elevator, down one hallway, then another. I stand up to leave, but she tells me to sit down. She wants to share all the other details. She wants to tell me about her third husband, who didn't really die. Who did some bad things to her. How she is always tired now, but for who knows what reason. The doctor thinks it is just because she is old. She's in her 90s. Sometimes her sister calls, but the sister has kids and other things to worry about. The nurses aren't so nice to her, she whispers. Her three husbands, though, are waiting for her in heaven.

"At least I'll have my pick," she says, and we laugh again.

But we keep coming up against the hard edge of her bad luck. Instead of family to visit her, there is this sparse flow of volunteers. Today there is me.

"That is the life," she says. "*Nos vamos, nos vamos.*"

We go where we go.

119

The Spanish reminds me of my grandmother, who is getting older too, was also an immigrant, and is now far from family. A similar vulnerability, but also a similar resilience. It almost feels like I'm sitting across from her, and maybe that's why I linger as long as I do.

"Be a good boy," she says before I leave.

Sometimes I think about the two cars, the three husbands. She always wanted to come to America. It was her dream to go. But the first husband always said no. That was it, end of discussion. Then the two cars collided.

"There was no one to say no to me anymore," she told me. "So I went."

JULIENNE

You hand me the knife. I am slicing off the skin, but the blade is dull. It takes focus, a particular angle. I fluster easily in kitchens. You keep asking questions and I am so distracted I answer without filtering. I just surrender the raw hurt. We've traded sadnesses before, an unexpected end of a promising fling, a biting criticism, a shitty turn at work. But last time when I told you something, your response was different.

"Yikes."

I don't mean to allow you the chance for another wound, but I am so busy trying to slice the onion, my defenses are not active. I try to slow it down. I ask about your job, but you outflank me. I have already given you something to go on. The follow-ups begin, and I ignore the reflection in the fast-moving metal.

"No, he didn't mean to be cruel," I say, not wanting you to have a poor impression of a co-worker who in the past I have spoken of in glowing terms.

I am not ready for this public alliance to disintegrate in your eyes. Then it may crumble for me too. I am right next to the oven, and I start sweating. I've revealed more than I wanted to. I am crying, involuntarily, from the onion. I am so distracted cutting I even tell you the worst of it. This is the way the story slips.

THE KING OF THIRD PLACE

When he was younger, my brother always beat me in chess. He knew all the strategic opening moves, the arcane jargon. *Stalemate* the word for a tie, *en passant* a special way of capturing a pawn, *blunder* a crucial mistake. He could crush me even though I'm five years older. It was his thing, and he'd play in New York City tournaments. Once, I saw him lugging home a huge trophy with a stern-faced golden king on top. From far away in my room, it all looked pretty good. The trophies added up, and soon the first king had company. But in his room, my brother is getting really frustrated. Every single tournament he gets third place.

His eyes are fixed on first. Even second. Eventually he quits because he is tired of pushing this particular boulder. Forever in third.

"Third place in the city is amazing," I tell him, but he doesn't listen.

I still see my brother as a chess master even though he doesn't play much anymore. In the game, you can always rely on a rook to be a rook. A knight to be a knight. But the gridded universe is a simpler one. When we play now, I can beat him: he's not as good as he once was.

I like bringing up chess to covertly prod him. I want him to get back into it. He used to be such a strong player. We're sitting around bored at a family gathering and I ask him which chess pieces he thinks correspond to the personalities of people at the event.

"You're the bishop because you think you're really powerful but you're not," he says, and we laugh and laugh.

Years pass, and sometimes we play. Only occasionally. I don't press it because I know it's not fair to pin someone to something they used to be. But behind the scenes, I hold on to my obscure dream about my brother getting better again. It somehow represents more than just chess; life seemed kinder to him then. He is the only person I can honestly say I hope beats me. I hope he crushes me. Takes my queen and forks me into a shallow grave. He's my little brother and we are eternally on the same team.

One day he calls – he's coming home for Thanksgiving in a few days. He's saying that he miscalculated, that he could've come home earlier, since he had less work than he thought.

"It was a huge blunder," he says.

I smile to myself.

MAGICAL DAVE

Everyone is a hulking six-footer except for someone they are referring to as Magical Dave. He looks at least 80 and has worn his moccasins to what is supposed to be a competitive weekly basketball game. He seems drunk, but I learn later that he's a health nut.

We're playing on Fire Island, a strangely shaped piece of land that is 31 miles long but only 160 meters wide in some parts.

I'm small, so I'm guarding Magical. They call him that because he somehow never misses a shot, despite his advanced age and limited height. He makes it in a particular way too, always a swish, seemingly without looking at the basket. In pickup, many people don't care about defense. They allow themselves to rest, to be lazy, to let offense dictate the game, but this is where I come in. I am all over Magical Dave, who's annoyed but also amused.

"You're like a cloak. I can't get you off me," he says.

He has to work for it, but he still makes some shots. I am scoring too. I am playing better than I usually do, and all my shots are going in. He tightens up, gets close.

"Givin' you a little of you," he says.

I make a fake move and start cutting to the basket – it is obvious I will get an easy layup. If I were taller, I would dunk, but Magical hooks his foot into mine, and I go flying, cement ripping my palms. I have just gotten over a sprain, and I can feel it now – I've sprained the same ankle. I am in serious pain, but I keep playing since my new boss is there, and it is the first time he's seen me play. Later, using a metaphor for my contributions to our magazine, he will refer to me as a scorer. He will say that you shouldn't underestimate this guy. He will act like I have a new depth he hadn't seen before.

I hobble around, but I still am scoring in what feels like one of my all-time greatest games. Magical is saying that I must not be hurt so bad, since I'm scoring so much. But then, he sees. My movement slows, my face looks different than before. When the ball bounces into the bushes, there is a lull and he comes over to me. I am somehow not so mad at him, even though the second sprain will lead to tendinitis in my knee and I won't play sports after for over a year. He tripped me, but he noticed me too. *The Cloak*. Magical Dave lets me believe in that story I tell of myself: *A fiery guard with a mean streak.* Maybe there's something to that nickname of his after all.

It turns out he is just as intense as I am. He gets real close. Way closer than I would normally be comfortable with.

"If I could," he says, "I'd feel your pain for ya."

TIME FOR A HAIRCUT

Even now, I'll make time. I push things off, I'll reschedule. I am available. L. and I are talking again, but she needs to give herself permission. Sure, we can talk later, she says: "I'm doing some laundry, so I'll have time."

It seems like there always has to be a reason, a blank space. It's the only place I can fit now, these banal crevices in her life. We rarely discuss things directly, because they're too fragile. She mentions she might be in New York for a weekend, might go with her family, but the next time we talk, it sounds less likely to happen. I read somewhere that the oldest definition of a stranger isn't *someone you don't know*. It's *someone who's stopped visiting*.

"I thought you said it was time for a haircut," I remind her, as we negotiate the forbidden topic of seeing each other again.

She likes a place here, from a summer two years ago. A summer with me. At the time, we spent an hour discussing all the reasons why it wasn't a good idea for us to be intimate again. Then we kissed. We met up in different neighborhoods, slowly taking each other through the city. We sipped soda in Bryant Park. We sat on the ground by the Barclays Center when all the benches were full. We sketched in an empty cafe until it closed. At the last minute before her bus left for a new city, we agreed that even though she was moving again, we could just call it a break. No "up." But she thrived there and our plan didn't make sense anymore. Now what she remembers about New York is its heat, the dirt, the insects in her room at night, the scary street she lived on.

She remembers she said she might visit and I am able to move her toward maybe.

"I do need a haircut," she says, as though she is measuring the strands, long and black, measuring their length in her hand.

WHY YOU SHOULD NEVER TRIP
WITH SOMEONE YOU BARELY KNOW

Someone will give you that advice and you will ignore it because you'd like to try mushrooms. You will go into an area of the city you've never been, far in the east. Notice that the house is furnished with golf trophies pilfered from the neighbor's dumpster. You are not high yet: every plant in the house is in fact dead, drooping lifelessly. You will have a hard time understanding that this is just the strange reality. Hours earlier, you bombed an interview where they didn't even bother asking you to decipher the third logic problem in the set; they had what they needed. Shrug off the fact that your host is more of an acquaintance – you've been struggling lately and this is something you've always wanted to do. When he "checks in" with you every two minutes to see how it's going, say you're fine but don't provide any other details. He wants something from you, but you don't know what it is yet.

You'll know the dosage is high enough when his face completely transforms, sprouting wrinkles that seem to be wriggling through the skin. Decline his home-made journals. He wants to collect your writings and sift through the intimate gleanings. To convince you, he will share some personal meditations such as "What is time?"

He will remind you he's guided many, many others through their first trip and is just curious how it's going right now. When you don't respond, he will seek more and more reports of you, but stay firm. Carve out a refuge by scribbling in your own notebook, watching as the ink seems to flow down the page like wet paint. Hear your own voice – really hear it. You will have some major realizations, but don't share them. Consider explaining but then realize you can't because every memory is temporarily snipped from your mind.

Try your best, but realize you will be a whole range of Jasons, sometimes really dogmatic and sometimes a babbling idiot. When your acquaintance tells you he's recorded forty minutes of your most unguarded self talking without your permission, ask him to please delete it. When he won't, decide you'll never trust him again. Sever any remaining interest you have in this person.

When you start telling stories again, abort them midway through because they are all stories you've heard about him. Someone will tell you to not take your phone with you because it's too tempting to text people and you'll "reveal" yourself, but decide at some point that you really want to check your phone. You are still trying to get over a breakup and maybe she's texted you. When you check, don't get too bummed out that the only new text is from your mom.

Be on guard. At some point he will put his hand against yours. He will not stop talking about how they are exactly the same size. Retract your hand to tell him you feel trapped. Press yourself into the couch. Hold your ground. He will inch toward you and give you an energy that confuses you. He will twirl a statuette he liberated from the dumpster between his toes. He will say one of his two rules is that "whoever you are underneath is okay." He will scoot toward you on the rug. He will take out the Kama Sutra and ask you how big's your dick. You should extricate yourself, but it will be hours before you get out, lost in what seems like an uncommonly large house, bloated with infinite rooms. Bike over to your ex-girlfriend's apartment but expect to talk mostly with her roommate, because she doesn't really love you anymore.

OUR CHAMPAGNE

I ask my high-school-age soccer players to raise their hands if they've heard of Alexander the Great. It's the only time all season I'm running practice by myself. Since the other coaches are indisposed, I can exert the full brunt of my influence. There is no one to say no. I make up a drill and try to teach the instinct of aggression through historical mythology. That sometimes in a game you won't be in a position to take a perfect shot. Sometimes if you have a chance to score, any chance at all, you need to just rip it right then. Just kick the ball without fussing around. I tell them the story of Alexander and the famously convoluted Gordian knot, how he just sliced it.

"Cut the knot," I'm yelling to the kids, like an educated idiot.

A player will tell the head coach later that it was a great practice, and I will fly on that comment for weeks.

As the field gets darker, an older kid no one knows asks if he can join. Sure. We do a penalty shootout and I am the faux announcer with an invisible microphone, turning them all into superstars for just one minute. A Lionel Messi with acne. A Fernando Torres with braces.

When the practice is over, the newcomer asks if he can talk to me for a minute. I am not really in a position to be giving advice. I have been forgetting who I am, some of the good things. There's no one to remind me. But he is arriving at a calm moment in a wild season. We are big time rookies. First year coaches in a school known more for academics than sports. Buses are missed, shin guards forgotten, uniforms unfunded. We have no permits, so we find small triangles of grass on the fields of other teams. Eventually we find somewhere to practice, but we shimmy through a hole in the fence just to get there.

At some point I'm talking to a ref and he is decrying the kinds of coaches who need winning to validate their whole existence. We are both early for the game, just us and the grass. He's put down his airport thriller to chat. I know the stereotype he's referring to – I am nodding because I know it, but also because it is obvious that it's me.

"I can't imagine you yelling," the girl I'm dating tells me.

In the C Division, we will start two and three and then win our next nine games. We will lose one of the coaches to another job. The two of us who remain will put more of ourselves, of our emotions, into the team than maybe any person should. We will create a community that kids still come back to even after they graduate. We will win the quarters, the semis. In the last minute of overtime we will win the title. We will storm the field, and I will experience a joy so pure it is hard to describe. Smoothing over every other thing. We will shake seltzer as our champagne. The bus home from Randall's will be a bus-sized seizure of our happiness. Even the M35 driver will be in on it, flicking the lights on and off in accompaniment to our wacky rap songs. We will speak of these moments to everyone we know.

Away from the other kids, when the practice is over, the player asks me his question. I am only there to answer it because my jobs are all part-time and going nowhere, and because one day when I am wasting away playing *Madden 14* on a weekday, my old friend calls me and asks, "You wanna do this thing?"

I am an assistant coach, not even listed on the league website. Officially, I am no one.

"How can I be like you?" the kid asks me in the darkness.

IX

THE RULES OF GETTING TO KNOW SOMEONE

We are sitting so close I can barely see her. We can't say anything because the park is having a show and the actors are right in front of us. We whisper. This close, faces have a natural gravity. When she looks away from the actors, I say, "You missed it." We are having a whole conversation in whispers, about schools and kids and studying Shakespeare in high school. There is so much I want to say, but I can't, we have to be quiet. But then we start talking again, because we are here. We came all this way so we could meet.

Over text she'd said she was cold, so I brought her my sweatshirt, a navy blue just blue enough to not be black – a birthday present from my mom. L. used to wear my sweatshirts, even though they were way too big. As we stand up to leave and move into the reality of the date, I hand it to her, but she puts it on backward. I'm charmed by this, though I have an idle thought that if she raises it, the hood will obscure whoever she is. I don't ask her how many siblings she has. She doesn't ask me what I do for a living. It is like we already knew each other, we are simply continuing.

•

It is a few hours before I meet her and I am in the Nogu-chi Museum. It is an empty day – I am wandering around Queens with myself. The museum is divided into areas. Area 1 is mostly vertical sculptures that look particularly pared down, almost like people – people who've lost something. I walk around and around, there's no rush, I have nowhere to be. I am really trying to look at the sculptures. I don't dare touch them. Instead, I rest my hand on the wall, which is surprisingly cold.

The thing is, people can't resist touching the stones, though you're not supposed to. Near me a young couple is waiting for the museum attendant to leave the room, to resume her rounds. When she does, they each put their hands on the stone. First he, then she. Quickly, as though it would scorch them if they held it for too long. They giggle and run to another room to compare notes, like it would be discourteous to talk about the sculptures in their presence. I love them for this. They haven't known each other very long, I decide.

I am texting her by now – I am telling her about the Noguchi Museum to tell her something about me. I tell her how people touch the stones, though they're not supposed to. This wins her over. Usually she likes talk-ing to someone longer, to vet them more rigorously, but she likes what I said about the Noguchi Museum. She is willing to break her rule. So much so, she decides yes we should meet, this same day, even. My phrase stands in for me, everything else omitted. The long days, the nothingness. My whole life is omitted except the Nogu-chi Museum.

I love Noguchi, the intensity of his quotations. It's fun pretending I'm a correspondent from a foreign country, observing the way of life in the museum, think-ing about this artist and things he once thought. They are

136

in every room on laminated display cards.

"I attack the stone with violence. Is it to tame it or to awaken myself?"

I wonder about him. About what happens to the rest of the stone.

I've already said I'd like to meet her; I don't see the point in so many phases of vetting. I don't think people are their words. People and their words are different things – the important thing is to meet. At first we text slowly, a day here, a day there, very slow. Today, a weekday, it accelerates. It escalates.

The museum is so silent it feels like it is just Noguchi and me.

•

The kids come. Big groups of kids, loud and wild. We are all in Area 3. A teacher is telling her young students to use their museum voices. She is telling them that because of me, because I am in the room too. But I am only in the room because I like hearing what the students have to say about the sculptures. I am reporting on the kids, via text, since she likes kids and so do I – we both work with them. The kids are less subtle than the adults. There is a black mound the kids don't understand, but they're curious. They kick it, nudge it, jump over it, test it. There is nothing the attendant can do but loudly sigh.

There is a sculpture that looks like a bench, that I mistook for a bench.

Even Noguchi says, "A seat which is a sculpture or a sculpture which may be sat on."

The museum staff asks us, *Please do not sit*, on one of their signs. I am certain they have good reasons for this, the wear and tear on the stone. Noguchi is not around to make another one, since he has been dead for nearly thirty years. The kids, though, don't even think about whether or not it is a bench. It looks like a bench, so they sit. The attendant is not always in the room, is not then. In Area 2, the teacher has instructed her students to draw some of the sculptures. The works here are very different, smaller and more horizontal and not so obviously made of stone.

"That one looks like a bone," the teacher says.

"That is a bone," say the kids.

"Keep looking until there are no more details," the teacher says.

I am still there, sketching but really listening. Taken out of context, her statement makes me wonder about seeing as an act of removal. Maybe I just forget she is only talking about sketching. When there are no more details, when you've given them all up, they aren't yours anymore. Your memory is no longer your own.

"We are a landscape of all we have seen," Noguchi says.

•

We are walking to the bookshop, the only one in the neighborhood. Side by side in the space of the sidewalk I can see her better. She's not exactly who she was up close. Sometimes on dating apps, what happens is that I'll get attached to a particular picture within the gallery. I decide that this one, the one I like best, is the reality, is what they truly look like. Like the others are aberrations. This is who they really are. But of course this is a lie, an illusion. They are all of them.

In the bookstore, we browse. For some reason I feel more interested in the browsing than in our conversation. She tells me about her books and I tell her about mine, the ones we've read. The overlap is surprisingly small. Not that mine are better, but our tastes seem so different.

I ask the attendant if they have a particular book. They do, but only one. Less than a minute later, a harried woman, very old, comes in. "I'm looking for a book for my book group," she says. She mentions the book I have picked, the book of which there is only one.

She can have it.

I know I am only buying it because I am in a bookstore.

·

We go to a bar with a lot of open space. Huge wooden tables. We only have an hour left, she tells me, since she has plans to meet a friend for drinks later. We sit side by side, because across feels too far away. We toast. I haven't eaten all day, but in a certain way, I am full from the museum, from all this activity. A few sips of beer and the malaise of the last few months feels like someone else's life.

I turn toward her and ask how she got in her life from A to B. She has a sketchbook with her, she takes it out, starts drawing and explaining. She asks what's made me happiest in the last month. She asks about something I regret not doing. I start drawing too. I've turned the page and we are both drawing diagrams of our lives. In spite of what people say, lives are long. She texts her friend, breaks her rule, cancels.

·

It gets later and the evening is gone – it is night. Darker, colder. We need to decide what to do. She says she's concerned about fast-forwarding, about going too fast. It's burned her before, she says. The faux intimacy that is sometimes borne out of comfort, the glaze of newness. I know the feeling too. It sounds to me like we're talking about sex without talking about sex. I shrug. We can do whatever.

"I'm very Go with the Flow," she says.

We walk back to my apartment, which isn't a short walk. I don't know what it is, but outside of defined spaces, things are laid too bare. Maybe there is less to disguise our lack of chemistry. I ask her a question, something about movies, and for the whole walk she can't answer it because she is thinking of something else.

Later, we are kissing and then she stops because she needs to know why I want to kiss her.

"I like how it feels. I like you."

She continues with the interrogations, like the whole thing is a word problem. It seems like there is a history here I don't know. All of a sudden, the way she sounds reminds me of a relative I don't like. I'm irritated that she's unwilling to suggest any songs to listen to. I have to pick all of them.

•

There is another man in the Noguchi Museum when I am there, who arrives around the same time. He takes a picture of every single sculpture; a completist. He only sees the sculptures through the lens, never once looks up, like the camera is a part of his face.

As a person starts to disappear from your life, time will whittle them down. Noguchi says about one of the sculptures called Torso that sometimes the fragment is better than the whole. At our table, when we are side by side, not across, when we are talking about kissing, about the feeling after a first kiss, she says that's when all the rules change, of how you can move and be and touch. This is my favorite moment of her.

X

NO ONE YOU KNOW

"They said maybe another hour."

"Did I tell you about the bullfighter yet? From reading about him, he seemed so devoted to his craft. Immersed in the pageantry, talked about it like it fed his soul. I just remember all this stuff about the purity of the thing. Then I heard the guy actually had a nasty coke habit, and he'd always do a line before the performance. Almost couldn't believe it. I guess I'd been taking the story as the whole gospel truth somehow."

"Yeah, it makes you think about all the things you don't know. That get left out."

"Do you think they'll ever be done? We've been waiting here for so long."

"What haven't we covered yet?"

"I think we got everything."

"Have you cheated on anyone?"

"No."

"You?"

"Yeah. A girlfriend I had in high school."

"What happened?"

"It was just something I wanted, I guess."

THAT NIGHT WHEN SOMEONE
OBSERVED SOMETHING ABOUT YOU

I am high and desperate to talk to someone, so I text huge swaths of my contact list. I text them variations on "How the heck are you doing?" but it is not enough; the replies are too slow. I take out my computer and start typing. I type a private Facebook message to a girl I knew in college who I was always friendly with but never quite friends with. Since I know we probably won't see each other again, I propose a series of candid messages about things we thought but didn't say when we knew each other. I always wished I knew her better. I am in St. Louis and she is all the way on one of the coasts.

She does not reply, for months. And then she does.

"I don't understand exactly how it works," she writes, addressing the stagnation in our friendship we both seemed aware of, "but I feel like one of the best ways to never get to know someone is to have them become a best friend of someone you already know."

In her email, she mentions a time we were all sitting on a balcony. Me, our mutual close friend she's referring to, her, and a few others. I am telling a story. Most other people there have been quiet, so I tell story after story. I feel safe in these stories because a story is after it happened; it's not you anymore. I am telling these stories, I am really in a groove, and then a shy exchange student interrupts me, chuckling.

"You really say 'like' a lot," he says.

I remember this moment well: I can't finish my story, so I eventually just abort it. I skip the rest. First I try to go on, but I say 'like' again and then again. I apologize.

"I think you think of yourself as a higher observer," my acquaintance writes in the email. "But that night when someone observed something about you, you seemed unusually caught off guard."

CATCHING UP

I'm at a party during an otherwise forgettable high school weekend. Someone's townhouse, people drinking. At the bottom of someone's grand staircase, I see a girl I used to know. Elementary school, Hebrew school. We come into focus.

"Something about you is different," she says.

I parry this by saying I just got a haircut, even though I haven't seen her in at least four years.

"Something's different," she says again.

I stand there, sweating and rattled, but she can't put her finger on it. I'm grateful when the rest of the night fades into Great to See You.

PRISONER OF WAR

I hide in Australia because maintaining any of the larger continents is too stressful. To go after them is to be spread thin; the other armies can easily penetrate my borders. As the games go on, I'm seduced by treaties, which benefit me less than they benefit my allies. In all the years the four of us play, I never have a distinct color. Sometimes I'm red, sometimes green, sometimes blue. I have no true identity on the board.

He's the best of us, with his gray pieces, the rebel. My friend behind the black pieces is the most aggressive; I always try to be on his side – he's the general and I'm the lieutenant. A 12-year-old manservant paid in the precious scraps of best friendship. Yellow is volatile. If you attack his territories too early, he will abandon reason and any semblance of strategy just to kill you, just to pull you off the ledge with him. In all the summers of my childhood, we play constantly in each other's houses, and I rarely win. My passive tendencies might as well be engraved in the board, invisible continents of my childhood.

Years later, at sleepaway camp, someone brings the game. Days are sports, nights are downtime. RISK generally starts with four to six players and lasts several hours. Most games don't reach their conclusion, but I win 18 times that summer. It's the same summer that someone suggests that my nickname on our bunk plaque should be *Huge Jewish Nose Schwartzman*. Kids make cruel comments about my appearance, even friends, and it becomes a fixture of my reality. In these years, I feel so small. In these years, I have no armor. Everything wounds, the words sticking in me like shrapnel from a never-ending war. But to etch that ridicule on a plaque? For it to be visible and permanent? It's more than I can bear.

Playing the game is its own reality. These kids don't know about my lack of a color, my losing campaigns. They just know I have played RISK a lot. I don't need to flee to Australia anymore. I take North America by the throat. I'm the black pieces now. I make up something called "non-aggression treaties" that aren't binding; I'm always the one to break them. RISK is a game with a significant element of chance, but that whole summer I lose just once. I keep track of my wins like a deranged accountant, as though to balance out my other losses.

As we walk through the woods one day, I'm arguing with my bunkmate. For some reason he wants that phrase on the plaque – he doesn't care how upset I am. He's actually insisting, gleeful, and I can't believe my friends stay silent. That no one sticks up for me. I become feverish and desperate, scrutinizing my bunkmate for vulnerability. I'm usually so incompetent at fighting back, but he's obviously overweight. Worn down and humiliated, all that's left of me is something vicious.

"How would you like it if we remembered you as *Fat Disgusting Cow*?"

He surrenders.

On the RISK board that summer, I'm always merciless. I don't even enjoy winning, I just want to not lose. If the latest residents of our bunk take a second to read our plaque all these years later, they won't see anything about my nose. They'll only see that I played RISK. That I won 18 whole times – that in a game of chance I lost just once.

I don't really play anymore, and I don't usually talk about the things I was called for all that time. I've tried talking casually about it, but inevitably, my heart races and I get hot and nervous. Words never seem to fully capture it, and I find myself almost immediately in a snarl of explanation, straining to convey how bad it was, then overexposed. I doubt myself for a minute, and then re-member, get sucked back. Most of the time there's no reason to say anything, and about that particular aspect of myself, I stay in an abstract Australia, the most remote and safest territory in the game, unless someone really wants to know. RISK takes a long time to finish.

IN OUR WORDS

I'm looking for a notebook, rummaging in a drawer, but the only blank ones I can find are from L. – she made them a long time ago, cutting out the paper and knitting the pages together.

It has been necessary to try and forget her, to wring her out of even the stories in which she appears, a person intentionally faded, detail by detail. To protect myself from seeing past the specter that now haunts these pages. From breathing life back into someone I used to know so well.

But when I see the notebook, I am reminded.

She made six small notebooks for my birthday one year. Three for her, three for me. We were going to be traveling together for the first time – the idea was to fill them up with what we saw, with what we thought about, to see what would happen. One of hers, she was going to give to me, she said. I'd always loved her drawing, her sketches, but I didn't have a single one.

On the last day, in Florence, she couldn't find her notebook anywhere – the one for me. She was sketching in it when we were down by the river; it was almost filled. She ran back to find it, but it wasn't there anymore. So soon, someone put it in their pocket.

"It's okay," I heard myself say. "I don't need the notebook. I have you."

For some reason she could not explain, a feeling she experienced ignited the flares of her memory, she wrote to me once about the minute we met. Something she heard in my laugh. She noticed and remembered more of me after that than other people she encountered. It wasn't as quick for me – we weren't quite on the same schedule then.

To her, words meant little. To me, they meant everything.

"They just fill a lack," she says a little after we meet, quoting Addie Bundren, a character from the one book she ever cared about, *As I Lay Dying*.

I'm disappointed this is the only book that imprinted on her, the only character even, but it turns out it doesn't matter at all. Despite what she says, the relationship progresses through words. While I'm ostensibly googling something on her computer, really I'm writing her a secret message on a dashboard sticky.

"I wonder if you'll ever find this," I write. "I'll try not to just tell you."

I travel to her room when she gets back at night and we talk. It's how we get to know each other, hundreds of little visits. Over time, we untangle different knots in her and in me.

I tell her that I feel a sense of inauthenticity, like I am lying just by standing here right in front of anyone. Something she says changes how I think about it – even now it makes all the difference. I think about that sometimes, how many people we have inside us, living in our words long after they leave.

Because of the surgery, I am able to breathe better. It helped me in so many ways, freeing me from something I was never able to speak about. So fundamental, so invisible because that's just how things were. But even though my nose is straighter, has no more bump, no more droop—

"It's a scar," she said.

REUNIONS

We are no longer little boys in the woodsy sleepaway camp of our childhood: we have put the bats and balls away, taken off our knee pads, stowed away our gloves, lost our Ping-Pong paddles. We are far from those summers in every sense: now we are crowding into a bar by Union Square. It is ten years later.

My best friend can't go, so I head over alone. I wonder if they'll even recognize me. I haven't felt this vulnerable in a long time: you never know what people will say.

The very first person I see yells out my name like he's spotted a species he'd long believed to be extinct: "Schwartzman!"

Two guys immediately reminisce about a basketball tryout where five campers were on the borderline for making the team. For the coach's final evaluation, he had us play a vicious, survival-of-the-fittest style game of basketball where no fouls would be called. What that meant was that you could be as rough as you wanted. No holding back. What they remembered most about me, the two guys explained, was how much I thrived in that element. The complete abandon. That younger Jason fighting savagely on that particular court in all his well-earned sweat.

Some of the people here I remember so well, small things they said, what tournament teams they made, which ones they didn't. But for some others I really have to dig deep, to rummage through all the drawers in my mental attic just for a single dusty photograph. Someone remarks that everyone looks exactly the same, but I'm surprised by how different everyone is. A thin guy is very heavy. A heavy guy is very thin. Some people who were annoying are still annoying. People who once gave rousing speeches are now just dudes yawning through boilerplate conversations. Seeing these same color war captains is unmistakably disappointing, like a soldier coming back from war and seeing his general working behind the counter at a local drugstore.

After just a few minutes, the heated excitement of ten years apart has cooled, and we are just guys in a room chatting. A member of the color war crowd calls me over; he works in marketing. He sounds effusive, but he also seems to be looking at me strangely. He's a few drinks in. The way he is looking at me reminds me of a nightmare I had once, that everyone knew about the surgery but wouldn't say. Others I had of not being recognized – a total stranger to people I know. Which has happened.

"You look really great," the marketer says to me at least two times, but in a pointed way.

My best friend has a memory much better than mine, and he says he can't remember the difference. He can sometimes recall a quip I made five years ago, but not this? At some point I realize it is not specific to me. Even when I remember younger years, I don't remember my friends as little eight-year-olds. I remember them as they look now, with their current faces and bodies superimposed. We are always updating and cleaning and polishing.

I can't tell if the color war captain is trying to tell me he knows or if he honestly thinks I look good all these years later, just processing a change at a reunion.

I have a feeling he knows. The funny thing is, he looks different to me too. He looks shorter than I remember.

By the end, I'm talking with a group of guys I didn't know well when I was a camper, who I know even less well now. I can't remember one guy's name, but it's on the tip of my tongue. All I can remember is that he was a hockey goalie – an impressive recollection, all agreed, especially because he wasn't so good. But neither was I. Wobbly on rollerblades, I was slow getting anywhere, and constantly stopping my momentum with an awkward screeching brake. Almost like I was lost, and a far cry from my freedom and intensity on the basketball court. Someone asks if I played hockey back then, the least popular of the camp's sports.

"Not really – I was a forgettable defenseman," I say.

And with *that* the goalie remembered.
"Schwartzman."

ACKNOWLEDGMENTS

This book made it into your hands thanks to the following friends and allies. Andrea Wagner provided Dear Sugar-levels of reassurance while answering all my late-night emails. Anytime we spoke, Dylan Murphy insisted that I keep sending my writing out, one last assist from our soccer days. Gabriela Britto gave an insightful read and boosted my confidence. Emre Sarbak helpfully scored every story in consideration from one to three in a trademark effort to systematize everything. Stephanie Kratschmer offered thoughtful notes and kept me steady with her friendship.

Jessica Granger relentlessly believed in me and made heroic efforts to corner agents at parties and inform them about "this cool book about strangers." It meant a lot how often Robert Schwartzman let me know he was still betting on me, even when the chips were down. Geoff Gray was generous enough to inflict on me all the editorial jabs and uppercuts in his arsenal; they have undoubtedly made me a better writer. Jon Roemer was the push I needed to roll this boulder over the hill at last.

I've been lucky to have had many wonderful teachers and professors influence my writing, most notably Sarah Morgan, Tom Sullivan, Andrew McCarron, Amanda Goldblatt, Jennifer Arch, Anton DiSclafani, Vidyan Ravinthiran, Danielle Dutton, Nick Reding, Bob Hansman, and Chloe Caldwell.

This book is dedicated to my mom, dad, and brother for their love and support. My mom taught me how to be kind and to notice the little things. My dad showed me that a good conversation should have a wild heart, and that there is strength in letting yourself be vulnerable. My brother is my eternal, loyal, hilarious comrade.

I owe Cody Zupnick a profound debt of gratitude for sitting with me in cafe after cafe, delivering notes through so many versions of the manuscript. His contributions were substantial.

Alexandra, I've saved for last. In the course of this book's journey, we started our own, and she became my most trusted editor. NO ONE YOU KNOW is much better having passed through her hands. Alongside the editing, something else was happening, and I wasn't feeling like a stranger anymore. My deepest thanks is to Alexandra, for making me feel known.

I also want to thank the editors of these journals and magazines, where some stories first appeared:

"The Shape of a Story": *Hobart*

"She Used To Be Someone Else Too": *Schuylkill Valley Journal*

"The Sheet": *Narratively*

"Streetball," "The Sweetest Shot," "Which World We're In": *Hippocampus Magazine*

"The Things That Fall Between": *Claudius Speaks*

"By Chance": *The Rumpus*

"Some Things You Can't Hold": *River Teeth*

"The Beep": *X-R-A-Y Literary Magazine*

"The Man on the Street": *Untapped Cities*

"A Matter of Meters, Miles, Roads": *perhappened mag*

"The Rules of Getting to Know Someone": *Human Parts*

ABOUT THE AUTHOR

Jason Schwartzman's essays and stories have appeared in the *New York Times, New York Magazine, Narratively, The Rumpus, Hobart, River Teeth, Nowhere Magazine, Human Parts, Mr. Beller's Neighborhood, Hippocampus Magazine*, and elsewhere. He is a founding editor of True.Ink, a revival of the classic adventure magazine. NO ONE YOU KNOW is Schwartzman's debut book.

CPSIA information can be obtained
at www.ICGtesting.com
Printed in the USA
FSHW011812130421
80447FS